Souls
Reborn

Vikings of Honor, Book Three

RENEE
VINCENT

SOULS REBORN
Copyright © 2017, Renee Vincent
Trade Paperback ISBN: 9781944484101

Digital ISBN: 9781944484095
Hardback ISBN: 9781944484170

Cover Art Design by Renee Vincent
Stock Art by BigStock.com
Editor, Linda Ingmanson
Digital Release: May, 2017
Trade Paperback Release: May, 2017
Hardback Release: March, 2022

Publishing History
First Edition of revised work published by Turquoise Morning Press
under the title *The Fall of Rain,* Copyright © 2011 by Renee Vincent

Second Edition of revised work published by Renee Vincent under the
title *The Fall of Rain,* Copyright © 2015 by Renee Vincent

For God, your presence in my life is constant and pure. Thank you for listening to my prayers and being with me every step of the way.

For my dearest grandmother, Lorraine, after whom I've named my heroine. You are greatly missed.

In Loving Memory of Lorraine
(1921 – 2010)

For Lindsey,
I can smile with deep satisfaction knowing I've kept my promise to you.

Praise for SOULS REBORN

"I didn't believe it was possible to take Daegan and Mara's incredible love story to another level, but I am extremely pleased to be wrong. The author is phenomenal in bringing to life the sights, sounds, and emotions through well researched descriptions and dialogue. Every word seemed to have a purpose in helping create a beautiful and poetic ending to an unforgettable trilogy."
—Night Owl Reviews

"This is one you will not soon forget! As Ms. Vincent alternates between the past and present, she brings both vividly to life in a way that only she can. This series has definitely made me a fan of Renee Vincent's works and is the reason that her books are now on my 'must read' list. Do yourself a favor and do not miss it!"
—Romance Junkies

"Renee Vincent weaves a tale of everlasting love that transcends the boundaries of time."
—Coffee Beans & Love Scenes

"I know for myself I enjoyed the first two books very much. So much so, that I was excited for the third book to come out. Little did I know what book three really had in store for me. OMG doesn't even cover it. This is my absolute most favorite book of this series!"
—*Romancing the Book*

"I was crying happy tears when I finished reading this book. Author Renee Vincent made this Dægan Lover very happy. I'm very happy how she ended this wonderful series."
—Viking Princess, Book Reviewer

"Captivating and breathtaking! I am overwhelmed with high emotions! I love this author because she pulls me into her stories with words that are flowing and keeps me interested until the end. She truly is a talented storyteller! I highly recommend this beautiful Viking series, you won't be disappointed! I devoured this book!
—N. Laverdure, Book Reviewer

"I could not read this book fast enough to satisfy my need to know. Vincent skillfully crafted a fine romance with paranormal elements; you will not regret this continuing story of a love which never died."
—V. Mallard, Book Reviewer

Acknowledgements

To Barbara. I could never ask for a better mother-in-law or for a more honest editor. We did this together!

To Teresa Fordice for helping name Lorraine's ex fiancé, Brad. It was a perfect fit, and I thank you for coming to my rescue!

To John Tracey, thank you for entertaining my characters with your lovely musical talents! One day, I hope to hear you live, in a pub in Ireland, instead of on YouTube. (Visit **www.youtube.com/JohnTraceyMusic** to check out my favorite acoustic guitarist from Belfast, Ireland!)

To Willie, Karen, Mícheál, and Catharina. You all are the best! I can't wait to see you all again. Hopefully, it will be in the near future. Until then, I will keep the memories we've made together close to my heart. Éire Abú!

To my undying loyal fans. I do hope you enjoy the modern version of Dægan Ræliksen as much as I have enjoyed creating the man who has medieval Norse warrior blood coursing through his veins. Long live the sons of Rælik!

And lastly, to Gregory, my knight in shining armor. Though it may sound cliché to some, that is exactly what you are to me. You've stood by me through thick and thin, and I'm honored you chose me to be your wife so many years ago. I look forward to living out the rest of my days with my own personal romance hero. May we live happily ever after…

SOULS REBORN
Vikings of Honor, Book 3

As if called by the object, Leif Dæganssen, an archeologist from Norway, uncovers an ancient chest buried beside his coastal cottage in western Ireland. The intricately decorated artifact might confirm the existence of a Viking settlement on Inishmore. Leif is driven to establish a link between himself and the Scandinavians who once inhabited the rugged isle.

For as long as she can remember, Lorraine O'Connor has had dreams of a Norse warrior. And even though she's never fully understood the reason, she welcomes the meaningless pleasure of being in a Viking's protective embrace—until the day she meets that very Northman on an impulsive vacation to Ireland.

Though blindsided by the relevance of her dreams and the eerily familiar man within them, Lorraine can't help but feel drawn to Leif. The more she gets to know him, the more she's convinced they've shared a life together in a time long forgotten.

As their pasts and present lives begin to intertwine, old conflicts and angers rise to the surface. Leif and Raine must win the right to be together in this life – if Raine can even convince Leif he was once her ancient Viking lover.

*Previously published as *The Fall of Rain*. (This new edition has been partially rewritten and professionally edited, along with a new title and new cover.)

Chapter One

Ireland, Present Day

Leif Dæganssen was soaked to the skin. The cool June rain beat on his back and thunder rolled across the heavens as he staked his shovel into the saturated ground outside his quaint Inishmore cottage. Normally, he'd never think of digging in the ground on such a terrible night. But every bone in his body urged him onward. He had no idea what he was looking for. His gut told him that something grand and unique might very well be hidden beneath his porch.

Leif was not a superstitious man. In fact, his livelihood as an archeologist never allowed him to consider supernatural practices. After years of schooling and countless, tedious digs, he only believed in things explainable through science, carbon dating, and the naked eye.

This was different.

He dug on a hunch, an innate feeling coursing through his veins. By rights, the storm should have slowed his progress, or at least made him think twice on the idiocy of this escapade. But the dousing Erin rain fueled a fire so great that he ignored the aching muscles in his back and arms. The more it drenched his clothes, the more he was determined to scoop the dark, sopping mud away from his lattice-enclosed porch. Shovelful after careful shovelful, he dug away the soil, ignoring the long heavy sighs of his younger brother, Kristoff.

"How long are we going to be out here in this storm

digging for worms, Leif?"

Leif paid him no attention. He concentrated on the depth of his ditch around the front of his house and the silent calculations he made in his head. The perimeter hole he had already dug was about two feet deep, and he knew the topsoil would eventually give way to rock-solid limestone beneath. A few more inches—at max maybe another foot—and he'd find something.

He could feel it.

As sure as the rain dripped from every strand of hair in his face, he could feel his adrenaline rising at the thought of his shovel hitting something solid.

"Leif!" Kristoff yelled, jerking him by the arm. A flash of lightning ripped across the midnight sky. Both flinched at the heart-stopping crack and peered above. Kristoff turned his attention back to his brother. "This is insane. We're going to get killed out here."

"Then go inside," Leif said. "I'm not quitting."

"And I'm not letting you get struck by lightning over some stupid gut feeling for an artifact that may or may not be here."

Leif squared his shoulders and leaned in close, the rain spitting like needles in his face. "I'm not stopping," he repeated, driving his shovel deep in the ground. A low, dull thump thudded back. "Did you hear that?"

Kristoff looked at Leif skeptically. "I did…"

Leif's face lit up brighter than the violent streak of lightning that passed overhead. "I told you I'd find something." He dropped to his knees, throwing his gloves aside as he dug beneath the last bit of mud. Against his training that called for careful excavation, he tore away handfuls of soil. Within seconds, his fingertips scraped against something solid.

"I feel it," Leif said breathlessly. "It's right here." Like a dog pawing for its buried bone, he dug until the top could be seen.

"Holy Halfdan Haroldsson," Kristoff mumbled as he saw a distinct pagan carving come into view. As the rain washed it clean, a whole slew of carvings took form before their eyes.

Leif glanced at Kristoff. "Now, do you believe me?"

"I do now. Come on, dig it out."

Leif didn't need his brother's encouragement. For years, he'd been trying to convince Kristoff that this Irish island was the home of their Norwegian ancestors. More importantly, that the house he had bought two years ago was likely sitting atop their settlement. He had no proof. Only a vibe he felt from the moment he stepped foot on the treeless island.

Until now.

Even in the dark of night, through the shroud of Ireland's merciless rainfall, there was no mistaking the Scandinavian carvings on the wooden artifact. They were telltale coils of a history forgotten—instantly recognizable designs spiraling and twisting into a complex weave of creatures, demigods, and beasts.

To a young archeologist, it was like striking gold.

"What do you think this is?" Kristoff asked as he helped to dig.

"I don't know. Perhaps a shield…or a weather vane from a longship."

"No," Kristoff said, peeling away hunks of mud from the side. "I think it's thicker than that."

Their excitement vaulted in unearthing the sizeable object from its grave. Words escaped them for guessing what they thought it could be, but one thing rang true. It was a large find—literally.

In the archeological world, antiquities such as a small coin or a glass bead were significant discoveries. Most times, they were found purely by accident. Then, once the find was made public, archeologists from all walks of life would try to establish the site as historical and gather funding for a further, more intensive dig. Finding anything beyond the small artifact took months or even years of dedication and meticulous excavation with skillful hands. Leif had found something substantial within a matter of minutes, and it was certainly nothing short of impressive.

As he and Kristoff lifted the heavy wooden relic from the mire of his crude excavation and set it on the grass in silent awe, they stared at the highly decorated object with its complex loops and spirals making up the elaborate, dated designs. This was no accident. This coffer had called to Leif—had beckoned him to buy this property. Though it proved nothing about his ancestors specifically settling here on this very spot, it did confirm that someone of Scandinavian descent had visited the isle. He was determined to find out who and hopefully link them with his Norwegian ancestors.

Gazing at the stunning carved box through the pelting rain, Kristoff broke the silence. "We're going to be famous."

Leif shot his brother a grave look. "We're not telling a soul about this."

"Are you out of your mind? Do you not know what this is?"

Leif ignored him. All he wanted to do was take it inside and get it out of sight, but he lost his footing in the slippery mud hole and fell on his backside.

"Here," Kristoff said, thrusting out his hand. "Let me help you."

Leif accepted his brother's aid, then hurried up the steps of his front porch, carrying the heavy box. Kristoff navigated past him and opened the door wide so he could pass through with ease.

In the dark, he walked straight into the open space of his living room and into the adjoining kitchen, where he set the object on the table. His heart hammered at the excitement of finally seeing his find under overhead lighting.

Stepping back, he reached for the switch on the wall, unable to tear his eyes from the dark object displayed on the table. He heard Kristoff's heavy footsteps approaching, but he didn't have the strength to flip on the light.

"Turn it on already," Kristoff demanded.

"Not yet."

"What do you mean, not yet? Turn on the light."

Leif studied his brother in the dark. "Kristoff, you must promise that what we see stays between us. No one is to know what we've found. And I mean no one."

"Why?" Kristoff asked. "We found something highly prized, and we could—"

"We're not going to tell a soul," Leif said. "If we reveal what we've found here tonight, this place will be swarming with media, treasure seekers, and museum enthusiasts. My home will no longer be mine and my life's work will be ruined. I've spent countless hours tracing our ancestors to this isle. And this...*this*," he said, gesturing toward the table, "could very well be the missing link to finding our distant family. Please, Kristoff. Don't spoil this for me. Don't take away my one chance of uncovering our past."

Leif heard his brother heave a heavy sigh. The moments ticked away with each drop of water on the cheap linoleum floor as he waited for Kristoff's response.

"Fine. I give my word. I won't tell a soul. Now turn on the bloody light."

Leif flipped the switch, but nothing could have prepared him for what he saw. It wasn't just a carved artifact sitting on his table above a puddle of muddy water on his floor, but a chest—a coffer that quite possibly held more riches than one man could fathom in a lifetime.

Chapter Two

Kentucky, USA

A billow of dust trailed behind Lorraine O'Connor's midnight-blue 1975 Corvette as she sped down the winding gravel lane and parked in front of Patrick's garage. At the sound of her slamming door, he stood from his stooped position, letting his horse's hoof slide from his dusty chaps and onto the ground. He leaned against the animal's hindquarter and patted its rump.

He watched his childhood friend march up the steps to the back entrance of his Cape Cod home and disappear behind the sliding glass door. Though Lorraine never glanced toward the barn, he knew by the resolve of her feet hitting the pavement and the hard draw of the door, short of shattering his glass, that something had gone terribly wrong.

"Looks like you're only getting the front shoes on today, Mr. Pride," he muttered to the horse. A slight smile tugged at the corner of Patrick's mouth. He couldn't help it. If something had gone awry with Lorraine and Brad on their Sunday afternoon picnic, then that would mean she was free from Brad's control. At least until they got back together again.

Oh, how he hated that asshole.

Brad was Lorraine's fiancé, but he certainly hadn't earned that title as far as Patrick was concerned. On more occasions than he could count, Brad treated Lorraine like dirt, often bringing her to tears. Then, he'd turn it around and make her feel as if she were the one to blame. She'd apologize like she always did and do something grand to make up for it. Being an only child and spoiled by wealthy parents, Brad would take advantage of her generosity, never thinking twice about the amount of money she'd spend on him. Lord knows she couldn't afford it. But that was Lorraine.

Many times, Patrick tried to talk some sense into her, to make her realize that Brad could never give her what she truly deserved. Lorraine would shrug and defend Brad with excuses Patrick never bought.

What had really upset Patrick was when Lorraine's parents both died in a tragic car accident last year and Brad had the gall not to attend their funeral. He claimed funerals were too difficult for him.

That was the day Patrick had stepped in. He had to. She was heartbroken and lost. Since she didn't have enough money to keep her parents' house, which the O'Connors had mortgaged twice, he suggested she move in with him. He hadn't really expected her to accept the offer of living on a hundred-acre Kentucky horse farm, but to his surprise, she agreed and had been living there ever since.

Much to Patrick's disappointment, Lorraine never dropped her pathetic fiancé. The only thing Patrick liked about the guy was that he couldn't seem to commit to a date, keeping Lorraine on hold until he was ready. Or, as Patrick assumed, until someone better came along.

He unbuckled the worn leather farrier chaps from his waist and calves and hung them up on a hook inside the barn. He stretched the aching muscles in his lower back and removed his cowboy hat by the brim, swiping his sweaty brow with his forearm. After returning Mr. Pride to his stall, he pulled his cell from his pocket. He hated to make this call, but it was necessary. Everything was necessary when it came to Lorraine, even if he had to disappoint his girlfriend—again.

He dialed her number and waited, dreading to hear Beth's voice on the other end.

"Hey, sexy," Beth hummed. "You ready for our ride today?"

Patrick absently kicked at the gravel in his drive as he left the barn and looked up into the bright summer sky, unsure how to respond. "About that…"

"Are you serious? You're canceling on me again?"

"I'm not canceling on you, Beth. I just have to take a rain check." Even as he spoke the words, he cringed at his pathetic excuse. It sounded like something Brad would say.

"Tell me you're not rearranging our date because of Lorraine. Tell me you just got a call for an emergency shoeing in Lexington. Anywhere. Please…"

Patrick stiffened. Blaming this on a high-dollar Thoroughbred sounded pretty good right now, but he wasn't the kind of guy to lie to his girlfriend. "I'm sorry, honey. She just pulled in like a bat outta hell, and evidently, Brad—"

"Why do you care so much?" she interrupted stiffly. "The best thing that could happen to Lorraine is if Brad would just dump her."

"I know that."

"Then let her stew for a while. Let her be pissed off enough to dump his ass for once."

"If I thought it would help, I would. But…" Patrick paced. He knew no matter what he said, Beth wouldn't understand. He cared for her dearly, but when it came to his relationship with Lorraine, he felt obligated to be there for her. He was all she had, especially after she'd lost most of her female friends because of Brad. And even if he kept his plans with Beth, his mind wouldn't be on his girlfriend, but on the fact he deserted Lorraine. It was best to just cancel his date with Beth and move on.

"Are you still here?" he asked.

She sighed. "Yes, I'm still here. But I can't guarantee it'll be for long."

"What does that mean?"

"It means I'm getting tired of being second best, Patrick. And I feel like you and I can't be together like a normal couple because Lorraine is always there. Coming between us. You need to get this sorted out and fast. I shouldn't have to wait at all, but I will, 'cause I love you."

Patrick smiled and hung his head. Those little words made him happy, but he never had the heart to say them back. "How about dinner at my house this Friday? You and me. No one else. We'll ride horses all day, and I'll cook for you when we get back."

"You promise? Just me and you?" Beth asked skeptically.

"Yes…" he replied in a soft whisper. "Just us."

"I'll be there bright and early."

Beth hung up before he could say anything more. He shoved his cell in his back pocket and rubbed the tension from his jaw with a stiff hand, mentally preparing himself for Lorraine.

****

Patrick stepped into the kitchen and slid the door

closed behind him. The house was strangely quiet and still. By now, his rowdy chocolate Lab should've been clumsily traipsing up, all tongue and legs, before he could take one step off the welcome mat. "Raine?" he called tentatively. "You in here?"

"I'm fine, Patrick. Leave me alone."

Lorraine's voice came from her bedroom down the hall. He kicked off his dusty cowboy boots and hung his hat on the hook by the door before making his way. As he expected, her door was shut, and when he gripped the handle, it was locked.

He leaned against the frame. "Raine, open the door."

"I said I'm fine."

There was anger in her voice, but through the gruffness she tried to fake, Patrick heard it crack. His heart melted. "Raine...talk to me."

"I don't feel like talking. I just want to be left alone."

Patrick rolled his eyes. No woman ever meant that. In his experience, *leave me alone* typically meant *be more convincing so I'll feel compelled to share my feelings.*

"Fine," he yielded. "I'll just sit out here and wait till you're ready to talk. I've got all day."

"Aren't you supposed to be horseback riding with Beth this afternoon?"

He rested his forehead on the door. "No, we changed plans."

"She changed plans or you did?"

He grew impatient with talking through the door. "What does it matter?"

"Dammit, Patrick, you can't keep doing that. You can't continue to rearrange your life with her because of me. She already hates me as it is."

Patrick tried the door handle again, to no avail. "Beth

doesn't hate you. She just doesn't understand my relationship with you. Give her time…she'll learn."

"She'll learn to hate you, Patrick. No woman wants to be second, and with me living here, you'll always put me first."

He caught the slight stress on "with me living here" and heard the closet door slide across its tracks, then the sound of her dragging something from inside. He pressed his ear against the door, listening. A zipper opened with furious intent and then a drawer from her dresser. "What are you doing in there? Are you packing?"

She ignored him.

"Raine," he demanded, his voice taking on an urgent tone. "Open this door right now."

She didn't oblige, and the longer he waited, the madder he got. If he knew one thing about Lorraine, it was that she was a determined woman. If she got something in her head, no matter how idiotic it was, she was going to see it through. He feared she'd decided to move out.

He couldn't let her. He cared too much to let her walk out of his life. The only place she could go was Brad's house in Indian Hill—the Beverly Hills of Ohio—and that was the last place he'd want her to run to.

"All right, that's it," Patrick warned. "I'm coming in."

He didn't know why he even gave a warning. It was his house, and he had a right to open any damn door he wanted. He spun around and reached above his bedroom doorframe for the pin key. He drove it in the tiny hole and burst into the room. Lorraine carried an armful of clothes to the edge of the bed, where a heap of unfolded clothes already lay in her suitcase.

His dog, Captain, jumped off the bed and ran to greet

him, paws and all. Correcting the dog, he pushed the animal aside and stopped Lorraine. "What are you doing?"

"Patrick, it's bad enough that I'm ruining my relationship with Brad. I'm not going to ruin yours too."

She tried to walk around him, but he stepped in front of her and clasped her face in his hands. "See? This is the shit I'm talking about. Brad has brainwashed you into thinking the reason your relationship is on the rocks is you. Do you know how absurd that is? Raine, it has *never* been your fault. Can't you see that? He doesn't deserve you."

"But Beth deserves you, and I'm not going to stand in your way anymore."

He grabbed her shoulders. "You're not in my way. You're my best friend. And I'm not letting you leave."

Tears welled in her green eyes. Her bottom lip quivered, and he pulled her into his arms, unable to bear the sight of her sorrow. "What happened?" He felt the jerk of quiet sobs in her shoulders as he led her toward the bed so they could sit down. Captain followed and lay down at their feet, his head on his paws.

Patrick took her hands in his. He noticed that the three-carat diamond solitaire she wore on her left, the only impressive thing Brad had ever offered her, was absent. Then again, Patrick never thought for one second that the man actually forked out his own money for it. He'd bet his life that Brad's parents paid for it simply because they didn't want their son to let a good thing slip through his hands.

"Where's your ring?"

Lorraine stared at the floor. "I gave it back to him."

Though her words were music to his ears, he restrained his joy. "Why?"

Lorraine blew out a tremendous sigh, and anger laced

her words. "Because I walked in on him with another woman."

Patrick's heart stopped. "With another woman…doing what?"

Lorraine glared at him. "What do you think, Patrick? They were in bed together, our bed—"

Her tears ran like a faucet now. "Okay, okay…" he consoled, pulling her against him. "I get it. It's okay. Shh…you don't have to say another word. I'm here." He didn't expect her to say anything more, but it was as though his words sparked a need to rant.

"You know what Brad did when I ran out of the house?"

Patrick didn't want to guess. He could only imagine what that scumbag did in the heat of Lorraine finding him screwing another woman.

"He chased me down the sidewalk with a sheet around his waist, saying he could explain. When I continued to run for my car, he actually grabbed me by the arm and said if I gave him just five minutes, he could be ready for our picnic." Lorraine began to laugh hysterically. "Can you believe that? He said he just forgot and double booked. Like I'm some insignificant appointment he failed to pencil in and scheduled a necessary fornication session in its place."

Patrick was dumbfounded. "Raine, I am so sorry. I—I…"

Lorraine looked up at him from the pocket of his shoulder. "Oh, don't act so surprised," she snapped, standing up to pace the room.

Patrick jumped up to embrace her again. "I know you can't begin to see it now, but it *is* better this way. You don't have to waste any more time on Brad. You're free to find the man of your dreams, the *right* man of your dreams."

"I don't think he's out there."

"Sure he is," Patrick contended, stroking her long dark hair. "He already visits you in your dreams every night."

Lorraine drew back to look at him. "You're talking about a guy who's a ridiculous figment of my own imagination, mind you, as if he's real."

"You've told me you could feel this man's lips on yours as real as if he were right in bed with you. You've had this dream ever since I've known you. So, how do you explain it?"

"It's called a pathetic girl's wish for her cliché knight in shining armor."

At that, Lorraine's cell phone rang, and she froze with a blank look. On the second ring, she scurried past him and frantically searched her purse on the bed. Pulling it out, she stared at the display.

She didn't have to read the name to Patrick. He already knew it was Brad. Infuriated, he grabbed the cell and threw it out of the room against the hall wall. The phone shattered in pieces, and before she could race out the door to salvage it, Patrick taunted his dog. "You want it? Go get it. Go get it, boy."

Captain jumped to his feet and ran to the plastic fragments lying haphazardly on the floor. Without even sniffing, he chose the biggest scrap and ran away with it in his mouth.

Patrick laughed, until Lorraine turned around with a scowl. She wasn't as pleased as he was with his dog's obedience.

"That was my cell phone. You broke it."

"I'll buy you a new one. With a different number," he

added. "Besides, you have nothing more to say to him."

"Says who?"

"Says me. Now start packing." Suddenly, her idea of leaving was the best thing she'd ever come up with. He was going to make damn sure Brad couldn't find her. "Pack your bags, Raine. You're going on a trip."

"A what?" Lorraine called after him. She watched him disappear into the hall, dumbfounded by what he suggested. *A trip?* Unable to stand there and be ignored, she jetted after him, catching up as he entered his office. He slid into his chair, and his fingers worked like mad over the keys.

Lorraine hovered over his desk and braced her hands on the flat surface. "What's gotten into you? One minute you're begging me to stay, and the next you're giving me orders to leave."

Patrick typed a few more words on his keyboard. "Ah, here we go." He looked up at her. "Would you rather leave from Cincinnati to Chicago to Ireland with a five-hour layover? Or fly into Philly with three hours to kill?"

She blinked repeatedly, her mouth agape.

"You're right," he decided. "Five hours is too long. Let's go with Philly."

"Patrick, you're not listening to me. I'm not going to Ireland."

He looked up from his screen. "Why not? You've always wanted to go there. And you would've by now had it not been for Brad holding you back. You finally have the opportunity to go whenever you want."

Lorraine straightened herself from the desk. "I'm not

going to Ireland. I can't afford it."

"I can," Patrick contended.

As he began to click around with his mouse, Lorraine grabbed his hand, jerking his cursor off the screen. "I'm not going, so don't bother booking a flight."

"Give me one good reason why."

"It's too soon. I'm not ready to be on my own. I've just spent four years with a man I thought I was going to marry, and figuring out how to be single again is not something I'm ready to tackle at this point. I don't even like the sound of it. The word 'single' to me means being morbidly alone."

"But you're not alone. You have me."

"It's not the same, and you know it."

Patrick stood and approached her, his face as serious as she'd ever seen it. "No one, at this very moment, cares for you as much as I do. I've sat back and watched you waste your life with Brad for years. I had high hopes for him in the beginning, but even he disappointed me in the span of a couple of dates. You've always known how I felt about him, but once you said 'yes' to his proposal, I figured there was nothing more I could do. You were a grown woman and capable of making your own decisions.

"However, now that you've seen the side of Brad that I've always suspected, you need someone who has a clear head, someone who can make decisions for you that are to your benefit. Believe me, darlin', you need this. You need this trip more than you know—if not just to distance yourself from Brad, then for the sheer enjoyment of it. You can do this. I know you can."

Lorraine stood there and listened to every word Patrick said. He was right about one thing. She definitely needed to distance herself from the man who broke her heart, even though she'd like to go back over to his house and give him a piece of her mind. As grand and exciting as going to Ireland sounded, she still didn't think she had the courage to go on her own. She could hardly stomach the thought of going to a restaurant by herself, much less journey to another country.

Patrick took her hands and folded them in his. "Would you rather I go with you?"

Lorraine rolled her eyes. "Beth would dump your butt for sure, and I'd never forgive myself." She heaved a heavy sigh. She didn't know how she'd gotten so lucky to have Patrick's undying loyalty, and the last thing she wanted to do was leave the only person who cared about her. "I don't know," she muttered. "I'm not up for a vacation right now. And then there's work. I'd have to take off, and who knows if I could on such short notice."

"You bartend at Molly Malone's. I think they can find someone else to serve Guinness for a few weeks."

Lorraine bit her lip.

"Come on, Raine," he encouraged. "What have you got to lose? There's nothing here to hold you back. You're as free as a bird. Grab those daring wings I know you have and soar the skies of Ireland. You never know…you might get lucky there."

"Let's get one thing straight, Patrick Owen O'Rorke. If I go anywhere, it won't be to get lucky."

Patrick's dimples deepened with his smile. "Never say never, Raine." Before she could say more on the subject, he slid back in his chair with his fingers readied on the keys. "So, is that a 'yes'?"

Last-minute jitters crept inside her as she contemplated her final decision. The more she thought about it, the more it sounded like an opportunity she'd be stupid to pass up. "Only if you let me pay you back."

"Whatever."

When he grabbed the mouse and gave it a click, her stomach instantly twisted in knots.

"It's done. You leave tomorrow."

Chapter Three

"Who's there?" Lorraine asked, peering into a dense row of hedges. She could've sworn she heard something, but no one answered. The cold hand of fear grasped her. She didn't have reason to be frightened, but she was. As she looked around, the feeling escalated. In front of her stood a thick forest of hardwood trees, and behind her ran a long winding river between miles of lush green meadows. Her surroundings seemed familiar, but she'd never stepped foot in this place before.

Suddenly, a man leapt out of the bushes and pulled her to the ground. Without much effort, he stifled her screams of terror with a simple hardened hand to her mouth and pinned her to the ground as easily as battling a child. But a helpless child she was not.

She had no idea why this man grabbed her and held her down, but she refused to cower to this brute and allow him to take advantage of her. She opened her mouth and bit his palm. When he retracted his hand, she launched her forehead into his nose, jarring him silly.

He collapsed upon her and trapped her beneath the weight of his body. She thrashed and tried to slip away, but he tightened his hold on her wrists. When she turned her head to avoid his bloody face, she saw an accumulation of men dressed in conical helmets and drab, woolen period clothing. They brandished their swords as they descended from dragon-prowed longships with red and white sails.

For a second, she forgot about the man lying atop her and gawked at the men—could she dare say Vikings?—gathering on the shore of the river.

The sheer sight of their immense numbers was enough to make her believe she was going to die at the hands of these menacing warriors. She'd seen plenty of historical reenactments from various Renaissance festivals in Ohio, but these guys looked and behaved far too real to be actors.

Finally, the man lying upon her lifted his head and regained her full attention. His nose had bled over his lips and down his chin. As he wiped it on the bear cloak that hung from his shoulders, he spoke to her. "I know you are frightened. But say not a word. Those men will hear you, and they will kill us both."

She looked at him, bewildered by his warning.

"I'll not hurt you," he whispered again. His beautiful blue eyes fixed on hers, and for a moment, time stood still. "You must believe me. I'll not hurt you. I give you my word."

Lorraine was utterly confused by the viciousness of his actions and the contradiction of his noble words. She knew nothing about this man, nor did his pledge mean anything to her. She wanted to get away from him, no matter the cost.

Realizing he'd loosened his hold, she brought her right elbow up to his nose again and hit it with such force that he yelled out and reached for his face.

Without delay, she pushed him off her and rolled out from under him...

****

Lorraine jolted awake the moment she hit solid

ground. Her head bounced off the hardwood floor of her bedroom, stunning her even more. In a panic, she looked around. There was no one holding her down and no Vikings surrounding her. Just Captain, who had padded into her room and began licking her face.

She pushed him away and sat up, her mind still hung up on the man who had pulled her to the ground. Though some things were a little fuzzy, one thing was clear—he was the same ruggedly handsome, blond man who'd been visiting her dreams for years. Normally, he left her with an unforgettable kiss. So, why did her dreams suddenly change?

"Are you all right?" Patrick asked as he rushed into the room, his strong arms already helping her to her feet. "I heard you yell. Did you actually fall out of bed?"

"I guess I did," she admitted, rubbing her sore temple.

"That must have been some kiss," Patrick joked.

"He didn't kiss me this time. I was standing in a meadow, near a river. He came out of the bushes and pulled me to the ground. I tried to get away, but he was so strong. And then he spoke to me."

Held by the facets of her peculiar dream, Patrick inquired further. "What did he say?"

Lorraine swallowed hard, reliving the terrifying moment beneath the man's heavy weight. "He said for me to keep quiet…else the men would see us and kill us both."

Patrick's eyes widened in disbelief. "What men?"

She looked at him and found it difficult to believe it herself. "There were hundreds coming ashore… Vikings." She watched as Patrick regarded her last word, his brow furrowing. "I know it sounds strange, but the men in my dream were Vikings."

Patrick attempted to rub away a smile from the corners of his mouth. "And was your knight in shining armor also a Viking?"

"I think so." She pondered for a moment, remembering the beautiful bear cloak hanging across his shoulders, his striking sea-blue eyes and golden blond hair. She also vividly recalled the blue kirtle he wore, the sword and scabbard at his left hip, and the small silver clips in his hair. Concluding that no one in this day and age wore tablet-woven tunics or bear cloaks, there was no doubt that he too was a Viking.

She glanced at Patrick and saw that he was grinning at her expense. "I know it sounds ludicrous, but I know what I dreamed."

Patrick wrapped his arm around her shoulders. "Maybe you *have* seen too many epic historical movies."

Lorraine elbowed him, but he didn't budge. He led her out of her bedroom and down the hall to the kitchen, going on about the last historical movie they'd watched together. She hardly heard a word as her mind focused on the strange dream and the man who had looked into her eyes with genuine urgency and concern.

"You hungry?"

Patrick's question and the smell of goetta and eggs brought her back to reality. She brushed her messy morning hair from her face and sat down. "I could eat."

"Good grief, Lorraine," Patrick said, heading straight for the freezer. He reached in for a bag of frozen peas and brought it to her. "You have a goose egg on your forehead."

She touched the painful lump and felt its pang beneath her fingertips. "Ouch. I sure do." Still stunned by her eventful morning, she took the cold compress of vegetables and gently applied it to her head.

Patrick crossed his arms and gave her a sympathetic smile. "If you were trying to get out of going to Ireland today, you could've just faked a stomach virus instead of concussing yourself."

"Ha-ha," Lorraine mocked, wincing in pain from crinkling her brow.

"Sip on some coffee. I'll get your plate ready."

Lorraine slumped in her chair at the head of the large country table, big enough for eight people, with Captain finding his usual spot at her feet. She drank the coffee Patrick had prepared for her and licked the whipped cream from her upper lip, indulging in the first taste of sweetness in her otherwise unpleasant morning.

"What time is my flight again?"

Patrick divided the scrambled eggs and goetta between two plates and carried them over to the table. "You have an hour and a half before we have to leave for the airport." He sat down next to her and placed the pepper shaker at the top of her plate before he took a sip of his own coffee.

Lorraine smiled inwardly at the gesture. It wasn't so much that he knew she loved pepper on her eggs. It was that he'd always been attentive to her likes and dislikes. Who would do that for her once she was in Ireland? While Patrick had contended that being single was a great opportunity to pamper herself, she feared it was a time to get acquainted with the many stages of loneliness.

"Oh, I almost forgot. I have something for you." He walked over to the counter and grabbed a small box wrapped in green-and-silver wrapping paper, complete with a bright orange bow. To most, it would be an unsightly combination of colors, but to her, it was beautiful. No one got her love for Ireland the way Patrick did.

He sat back down and slid it across the table. "Thought you might need this on your trip."

She looked at him, contemplating the contents of the gift, and set the makeshift ice pack next to her plate.

"It's not much, but I figured I owed it to you."

A small upsurge of excitement bubbled inside her as she pulled off the bow and unwrapped the box. "You didn't have to do this."

Patrick laughed as he took another bite of his toast. "Yeah, I did."

When she opened the box, she found a brand-new cell phone. She recalled the sudden death of her other phone and smiled appreciatively. "Thanks, Patrick."

"I've already got my number programmed in there for you, so if you feel the need to call me, just press 'two.' And don't even think of using this phone to call Brad. Right now the phone is still in my name, and if I so much as see his number on your itemized call list, I'm shutting it down."

Lorraine's mouth dropped open. "You don't trust me?"

Patrick stuffed his mouth with a goetta patty. "Nope."

She wasn't all that shocked. Hell, she didn't even trust herself at this point. Without Patrick by her side, she probably would've answered Brad's call last night and listened to his cheap apology. What's worse, she feared she might have even believed it.

"So, here are my rules while you're in Ireland," Patrick continued as he swallowed. "No calling Brad. No turning in before the sun sets. No wallowing in self-pity. And above all, do something crazy at least twice a week while you're there."

"Crazy...in Ireland..."

"I know it's not exactly Spring Break in Panama, but surely you can do something unexpected on the Emerald Isle. I want a full report the next morning when you do."

Lorraine had to laugh. She was never the type to throw caution to the wind. The likelihood of doing something foolish in another country was slim to none.

Instead of dousing Patrick's high hopes, she went back to drinking her coffee and eating her meal. It was better to let Patrick think she'd be daring, given he was footing the bill for this expensive vacation. To do anything less would seem ungrateful.

Patrick was the solid ground beneath her feet, her best friend—her only friend. No one could boast knowing more about her than he could. They'd shared so much through the course of their lives that being with him felt as comfortable as breathing. The only aspect of their platonic relationship they hadn't jumped into was the intimate part. Not that it didn't ever come up or that they never found themselves staring into each other's eyes for a few awkward moments before breaking away. It seemed inevitable that those moments would rear up from time to time, especially when two heterosexual friends lived under the same roof. But both of them seemed to be a little hesitant to make that leap for fear of ruining something special.

After taking the last bite of her food, she leaned back in her chair and pressed the thawing bag of peas to her head. She looked at Patrick, who was smirking like the devil.

"Vikings, huh?" he asked.

She scoffed. "And to think you're the one who kept acting as if this guy in my dream was real, not me."

"Who knows, maybe this Scandinavian is waiting for

you in Ireland. If I remember correctly from all those European history courses we had to take in school, the Vikings visited there often."

Lorraine knew Patrick's sarcasm was only meant to humor her. She rose from her chair and planted the bag of peas on top of his noggin. "I think you need this more than I do."

Chapter Four

Never say never...

Those words couldn't have held more meaning for Lorraine than the day she stepped out the front door of the Man of Aran Cottage on Inishmore. Never had she thought this day would come when she'd be standing on Irish soil.

Although born in the States from a German-American mother and an Irish-American father, she'd always felt a strong pull toward Ireland. It went beyond her Irish surname and the knowledge of having a great, great grandmother from the seaport village of Kinvara. Something deeper drew her to this country.

As she looked out over the rugged terrain of the island, she was right where she'd always wanted to be, despite her initial objection to Patrick's therapeutic idea. Thirty-six hours ago, she had dreaded this trip, feeling awful for the call she had to make to her boss at Molly Malone's and terrified of coming to a foreign country alone. But now, as she drew in a long breath of fresh, clean Erin air laced with a hint of sea salt, she felt free and uninhibited by the stresses of her dull American lifestyle. Patrick would be proud.

Ready to take on whatever Ireland had to throw at her, she checked the belongings she had packed in her backpack: a camera, binoculars, a tourist pamphlet, and a much-needed raincoat in case the weather turned sour. As far as she was concerned, the heavens could pour down around her, and it still wouldn't deter her from venturing out. This was Ireland. Rain came with the territory.

She smiled and took her first steps toward the one place she'd been dying to see since she'd flipped through a coffee table book about Ireland at a family physician's waiting room at the age of ten: the remains of the mighty Dún Aonghasa. She'd seen many pictures of it since then, but nothing would compare to seeing it in person.

It was only about a twenty-minute walk to the prehistoric fort and a few hours to tour through the outer, middle, and inner enclosures. As she looked out from her perch high atop the three-hundred-foot cliff's edge, a sense of wonder and awe overtook her. Stretching out her arms, she let the cool breeze blow through her hair as the sound of the roaring Atlantic crashed below. She breathed in, savoring this extraordinary moment of her life.

In Kentucky, the rolling green hills of summer pasture and the smell of clean country air was one of the highlights of the majority rural state. But if one wanted to smell the aroma of rain, sea salt, *and* dewy grasslands, Inishmore was the place. There was nothing like it. The breathtaking sight of the windswept island, the long-standing remnants of its past, the charming cottages, and the crushing waves of blue sea and foam were enough to make a person extend their stay on the isle, if not take up permanent residence.

Yeah, she could live here. She could see herself abandoning her ol' Kentucky home and starting a new life on the Emerald Isle. Her mind went even further, and she could see herself tending flowers in the window boxes of her whitewashed stone house complete with red shutters and a thatched roof.

A blustery wind blew past her and knocked her momentarily off balance, cutting short her thoughts. A familiar scent caught her attention. Crinkling her nose, she sniffed the air again, hardly expecting to smell it again. This time it was unmistakable. From living on a horse farm, she knew it well and loved that familiar fragrance of warm equine hide and soft, worn leather. But here? On Inishmore?

She'd seen many tourists traveling on bikes, mini taxis, and even by horse-drawn carriages. But there was no possible way for any horse to draw a cart over the rocky terrain of the isle once it left the paved road. There were too many rock walls dividing the land in random quadrilateral sections, not to mention the hit-or-miss tufts of island horticulture hiding the rest of the island's stones.

Bewildered by the easily recognizable scent, she turned around. A few yards from her sat a rider on horseback. He was a rather large man with strong thighs and muscular arms. His hair was as gold as the setting sun, with lowlights of dark auburn blending throughout. A deeper shade of blond scruff covered the sharp, angular ridge of his prominent jaw.

He was a handsome man and definitely not an Irish native. By the way he sat on his jet-black horse—proud and content—he wasn't a tourist either. He looked as though the rugged island was his, and he was its proprietor.

Then Lorraine swallowed hard and blinked several times to adjust her focus. The guy was also the very man from her dreams. He may not have been clothed in the medieval garb or possessed a broad sword at his hip, but he was, without a doubt, the one who'd sprung from the bushes and held her down.

Fear set in, and her heart pounded so hard against her ribs, she thought she'd vomit. She tried to step away and quietly withdraw from the cliff without him seeing her, but her legs wouldn't move. She swallowed back the god-awful sensation of nausea, hoping it would dissipate. The last thing she wanted to do was puke right in front of this guy and, worse, defile Dún Aonghasa.

She was overheating in her raincoat despite the constant breeze whistling in her ears. Her knees buckled and the ground spun. She threw her arms out to steady herself, but it didn't help. As she teetered, her gaze drifted to nothing, and a blackness seeped in from all around her. The last thing she remembered was the edge of the cliff and thinking that if she didn't fall backward, she'd plummet to her death.

Leif looked to his right, about to greet the woman in a flashy orange raincoat beside him, but she staggered as if she were trying to balance herself on a swaying tightrope. Her face was white and her eyes were wide.

"Are you all right?" he asked. *Seasickness.* That was what it was. So many of these damn tourists came straight off the ferry to Dún Aonghasa, then stared at the moving sea surrounding them, only to find themselves battling a bout of vertigo in the most dangerous spot they could put themselves.

He dismounted in haste. "I think you need to sit down."

No eye contact. No reply. It was obvious she was too far gone to listen to him and possibly on the verge of passing out. Just as he took a few steps toward her, her eyes rolled back in her head, and she collapsed. Try as he might, he couldn't catch her in time, and she crumpled facedown on the ground.

Coming to her aid, he knelt beside her and rolled her over. A hideous purple bruise on her forehead instantly caught his attention. "Bloody hell."

He checked for a pulse on her throat, and a sigh of relief washed over him. As he sat there, he couldn't help but notice the beautiful sight of purity and grace that lay before him. His eyes drank in the delicateness of her facial features, the fullness of her bottom lip, and the clean cut of her jaw that slipped into a graceful feminine neck. She looked so unlike the other women he'd known, and he found the differences to be refreshing.

Her hair was gathered in a reckless ponytail where a few locks had fallen loosely across her chest. He reached down and stroked the soft, dark tresses between his fingers. Then before he realized it, he lifted a lock of her hair to his nose and smelled it. At first, he swore he'd smelled that scent before, a unique aroma of spiced perfume and whatever shampoo she used this morning. But a rumble of thunder shook him from his thoughts. *What am I doing? This woman needs help, and I'm smelling her hair.*

Leif looked around him. Not a soul in sight.

It figured she'd have to pass out when all the tourists had already left for their next destination on the isle, and just when he thought about riding off for the visitor's center, another roar of thunder changed his mind. There wasn't enough time before the rain set in, and he was better off taking her to his home where she could be comfortable until she was well enough to head back to her own accommodations.

He carried her in his arms toward his horse and quickly realized whisking her away was not going to be such an easy task. He looked her over one last time, determining that her wounds were not life-threatening, and tossed her over his shoulder. Since he'd never done this before, he thought the whole thing through before he slipped his left foot in the stirrup, clutched a firm grip around the horse's mane, and threw a heavy leg up over the saddle.

As he settled in the seat and lowered her body to his lap, he wondered who she was. He knew many of the Irish natives on the isle, and yet he'd never seen her before. She was definitely a newcomer, and a vision of heaven in his arms.

More thunder shook the ground, and, just as he clicked his tongue to get Thor to walk, the rain poured down in sheets. He pulled the unconscious woman closer to his chest and kicked his horse into a gallop. Together, they tore across the craggy field toward his house.

Chapter Five

Kicking the door open, Leif slipped through sideways, careful not to catch the woman's head on the frame, then booted it closed. They were drenched to the skin, and all he could think about was changing into dry clothes and building a warm fire.

As he laid her on the floor near his hearth, he caught sight of his old bearskin cloak draped across the seat of his rocking chair. It was a family heirloom passed down for generations, but as smitten as he was, he'd offer her anything to insure her comfort.

After wrapping her in the thick pelt, he built a fire with a generous amount of turf logs stacked beside his fireplace. As he watched the flames catch and spread, he unbuttoned his shirt and peeled it from his body. He hated the feel of clinging, wet clothes, and no amount of living in Ireland had gotten him used to it.

In no time at all, the fire's blaze and the unmistakable smell of peat permeated his living room. He sat back on his haunches and gazed at the woman sleeping on his floor. Watching her sleep and wishing she'd come to was like waiting for water to boil. He decided his time was better spent tending to his loyal horse, who was still standing in the rain.

He grabbed his raincoat off the hook, but paused. With a tight grip on the door handle, he glanced back at her, and it seemed she'd already possessed a tight grip on his heartstrings. He'd no earthly idea why and forced himself to step outside, thoughts of her just a hair's breadth away.

****

Leif checked his watch. An hour and a half had slowly crept by since he returned from the barn and changed into dry clothes, and there was still no sign of movement from the brunette. He sat across from her on a straight-back kitchen chair, meticulously rubbing neat's-foot oil over every inch of his water-damaged saddle while he waited for her to awaken. Caring for leather tack could easily take a few hours, if one cared enough to do it properly, but a man could oil a saddle for only so long before it was overkill. He half expected the oil fumes alone would've been enough to rouse her, and when that didn't happen, it became clear the situation called for alternative measures.

He capped the bottle and stood to put another log on the fire, this time being less careful of the noise he made in the process. He then touched her shoulder and opened his mouth to call her by name, but realized he didn't know it. She'd gone down like a sack of spuds before he had the chance to ask her.

****

Lorraine moaned and slightly opened her eyes, finding it hard to focus. She saw the figure of a man before her, calming her with his soothing voice. *Patrick... It must be Patrick.*

Forgetting she was more than three thousand miles from home, she relaxed as his hands caressed her hair and his voice reassured her that she was safe from harm. It didn't sound like Patrick's voice, but she convinced her groggy self that she'd probably had another dream. She closed her eyes to his pleasant words, allowing the crackle of the fire to soothe her.

Wait. Patrick doesn't have a fireplace...

She tried concentrating on the sound. Perhaps it wasn't a fire. She opened her eyes again, blinking away the blurriness and squinting to join the double images into one. His face emerged from the haze; a sharply chiseled face with blond hair and kind eyes.

Blond hair?

Her smile disappeared instantly as she caught her breath. Once again, she was face-to-face with the man from her dreams, and it all came rushing back to her. She'd been standing on the cliff of Inishmore when she caught sight of him and his horse. Her world had spun with the threat of the falling over the edge, and the last thing she remembered was him dismounting and coming toward her.

But where was she now? Where had he taken her?

She quickly looked around. Nothing was familiar, save him. She felt extremely nervous and alone. Frozen with fear, she watched him stand and cross the room to sit on the couch. If he did so as a small act of kindness to make her feel more comfortable, it didn't slow her racing heart. His physical presence, no matter how far away he went, was still enough to terrify her. She gawked at him, though she had no idea what he was thinking or what he wanted from her.

The man was a monument of beauty and power, sturdy as the ground beneath him. He had long blond hair, a well-groomed beard, and skin darkened from the sun. His eyes revealed a sense of maturity and intelligence, yet even the darkness could not hide their color, for they were as blue as the ocean she'd crossed to get to Ireland.

"*Lochlannach*," she breathed.

He drew back. "You're Irish?"

Lorraine swallowed, wondering where that word had come from. She didn't even know what it meant. "No, I-I'm American."

"But you spoke Irish Gaelic and called me a Viking. *Lochlannach* means 'lake dweller'—a term the Irish called the Norse foreigners a long time ago."

Lorraine stared at him, still unsure of herself or what had come out of her mouth.

"It's okay," he said kindly. "It's not an insult as far as I'm concerned. I've been called worse in my time. Just didn't expect it." A smile tugged at his mouth. "I suppose the blond hair gave me away."

She wished that was what had given him away. Little did he know she'd seen him as a Viking in her dreams, and could barely wrap her head around the fact that he was real and talking to her. She sat up straighter and felt a strange dampness in her clothes.

"You'll have to forgive me," he began. "I tried to get you under shelter as quickly as I could, but by the time I mounted my horse with you in my arms, the rain poured from the sky. I would've taken you to your hotel had I known where you were staying, but I didn't even know your name. Is there someone you want to contact? Someone you're vacationing with to let them know you're all right? It's well after dinner. I'm sure they're worried sick."

His considerate words knocked her for a loop. If she had any residual fear of him, it had readily diminished. To know he'd picked her up in his arms and whisked her away on his horse just so she wouldn't get wet astounded her. Could he really be her knight in shining armor?

"Um...I'm staying at the Man of Aran Cottage. But I'm not with anyone," Lorraine clarified as she tried to stand.

Seeing she was a little wobbly on her feet, he rushed to her aid, bracing her elbows in the palms of his hands. "You came to Ireland by yourself?"

She blinked rapidly, her normal motor skills slow to react. In her delayed efforts, she staggered away from him.

"Here now," he coaxed, putting his arm behind her back for support. "You need to sit."

Lorraine looked up at him. His chiseled face was only inches from hers, and his large, brawny body hovered far too close, too quickly. She teetered clumsily backward. Before she could fall, he caught her and pulled her upright into his arms, her face smacking the warm blunt plane of his chest.

"Are you *trying* to hurt yourself? Because at the rate you're going, you'll be spending the rest of your Ireland holiday in the hospital." She flinched at the approach of his hand, but he stopped short. "Your head...you passed out. Remember?"

She touched where he pointed and winced. "Oh...right." Backing slowly out of his embrace, she offered a logical excuse for her unsteady behavior. "I'm just jet-lagged, I think. This vacation was a spur-of-the-moment kind of thing."

"Don't worry yourself. I'm just glad you're all right. Now, let's get you out of those wet clothes."

"I most certainly will not."

"Then how do you expect to gain warmth in sodden clothing?"

"If you think I'll remove my clothes simply because you ordered it, you're sorely mistaken. I'll do no such thing." I jumped from his arms and kept the hide for myself.

"Listen, princess," he said as he pulled off his boots and unbuckled his belt. "You, above all, should know this rain will hold us here for many hours, if not days. I'm not going to sit in wet, uncomfortable clothes when I've perfectly dry blankets at my disposal. And I suggest you follow my lead."

I hadn't long to contemplate his candid advice before he'd completely disrobed. I gasped and turned my head.

He laughed. "You might as well get used to it, my lady. Soon you'll be seeing me this way every night."

"I will not," I argued over my shoulder.

"Will you close your eyes to me, even on our wedding night?"

"You're a stupid heathen of a man! How can you possibly think that I'll want to marry you?"

"Excuse me? Marry you?"

Lorraine's eyes flashed open at the sound of a deep voice resonating behind her. She fully expected to look over her shoulder and see the man from her dreams completely naked in front of her. But when she peeked around, he stood there fully clothed, hands on his hips. A look of bewilderment filled his eyes.

"Don't you think I should at least know your name before you propose to me?"

Lorraine brought both hands to her head and squeezed. One minute she was talking about being jet-lagged in this man's living room, and the next she was watching him remove his wet warrior clothing while demanding she do the same on account of rain. It all seemed like a dream, yet she clearly wasn't sleeping.

"Is it still raining?" she asked curiously.

The blond stranger narrowed his eyes. "It is...which is why your clothes are wet, and why I suggested you remove them and get into dry ones." He quickly pointed behind him. "In the bathroom, down the hall, of course."

Relief washed over her. "I'm sorry...I'm...um..." she stuttered, words failing her.

"Are you sure you're all right? There's a doctor who lives up the road from here. You might be suffering from some mild head trauma."

"No," she said at once. "I don't need a doctor. I'm fine. Really." He didn't look convinced. "Look, I just need a moment to gather my wits if you don't mind."

"Sure." He reached for the pile of clothes from his coffee table and handed them to her. "I know they probably won't fit you, but they're dry. And I found a pair of pants with a drawstring, so that might help. The bathroom's two doors down on the left."

"Right. Thanks." As her cheeks flushed with heat, she accepted the clothes. But he didn't let go of them. Instead, he cocked his head.

"So, why am I a heathen again?"

A nervous laugh fell from her mouth. "I don't know where that came from. It was an outburst. It's obvious you've been nothing but kind and gentlemanly. I'm sorry if I came off as rude."

His gaze played over her, toying with her already scrambling mind. She'd never seen such a brilliant color in a man's eyes before, and it was hard not to drown in them.

Finally, he let go and reached for her backpack sitting on his couch. "Trust me, you didn't come off as rude," he said, handing over her things. "But you did give me too much credit with that 'kind and gentlemanly' nonsense. You might not think that come morning."

Lorraine recoiled, not sure what to make of him.

"Joke, love," he amended, then crossed his arms. "You know, for an American woman, you sure are a bit uptight. I promise, I'm not going to hurt you."

She couldn't recall a time when she'd been more embarrassed. All she wanted to do was escape. Sneak out his bathroom window, if he had one.

As he ushered her down the hall, she held fast to the clothes and backpack, recalling the strange vision as though she were living it out in real time. Then she felt the slight brush of his chest against her back when he leaned in and flipped on the light for her, and she swore she'd felt that closeness from him before.

Yes, that crazy notion confirmed she'd hit her head harder than she thought. This man might have resembled the brazen warrior in her dreams, but she had to start realizing it was purely coincidence. Nothing more.

He was a beautiful man, probably the most beautiful man she'd ever laid eyes on, and she hated that she'd acted like an absolute idiot in front of him. By now, he had to think she was a ditzy American tourist and probably couldn't wait for her to leave.

She backed up into the bathroom and started to close the door, but he stepped in and pointed to the handle. "The lock works on the door if you feel the need. Holler if you need anything else and…try not to fall off the toilet."

She closed her eyes and sighed. *Yeah, he thinks I'm a royal dumb-ass.* "Thanks." She shut the door, glanced at the lock…and turned it. Every muscle in her body finally relaxed, and she breathed a heavy sigh.

Alone at last.

Lorraine sat on the edge of the bathtub and rummaged through her backpack, searching for her cell phone. Because of the time difference, she never put a call in for Patrick that morning and knew she needed to call him now before he got worried. In addition, she wanted to hear his voice. She hoped he could help her make sense of her day. He'd always been her safe harbor, and right now, she could certainly use a calming dose of reality.

She used the speed dial option he'd programmed for her ahead of time, inwardly thanking him for being so conscientious. After the day she had, she doubted she could even remember his number, the one she'd known for years.

Upon his cheerful "hello," she sighed again and smiled.

"It's about time you called me, Raine. I was beginning to worry about you."

"I'm sorry. I didn't want to wake you this morning, and then I got caught up in sightseeing—"

"Too busy to call your best friend now that you're in another country, huh? I see how you are."

"It wasn't like that—"

"Chill out. I'm only teasing you. So, how's Ireland?"

"It's lovely. Better than I could've imagined," she said as cheerfully as she could muster. "I'm staying at the Man of Aran Cottage you suggested."

"So, what's wrong?"

Patrick was good. He was always perceptive even when she pretended that everything was all right. She swallowed, not knowing where to start.

"Talk to me, Raine."

She stood and paced the bathroom. "You remember that dream I had, the morning I left?"

Patrick scoffed. "You mean the one with your dream guy in Viking clothes holding you down on the ground? Yeah…what about it?"

She paused, finding it hard to explain the rest. "What if I told you he's here. On Inishmore?" Silence followed. The only thing she could hear was a long, thought-provoking inhale.

"I think you've had too much to drink at the pub, Raine. You best leave now before you feel it in the morning."

"I'm not in a pub. I haven't had one drop of alcohol."

"Okay, so you're tired," he reasoned. "You had a long flight last night and you haven't caught up after an exhausting day of sightseeing. Just close your eyes and go to sleep—clear your head. I'm sure you'll feel better in the morning."

"Patrick, listen to me," she whispered loudly. "The man I've dreamed about for years is here. On this, I'm not mistaken. But…" The next part of the story had her stumped. How could she explain zoning out and arguing with the man about wet clothing and marriage, if she could hardly believe it herself?

"Raine? You still there?"

"Yeah, I'm here."

"You cut out. You were saying you weren't mistaken about the man, but…"

Lorraine tried her best to put words in place of what she saw. "Do you believe in past lives?"

"As in reincarnation?"

Lorraine sighed and rolled her eyes. "Oh, it sounds even more ridiculous when *you* say it. Just forget it." She ran her hand through her tangled hair and glanced at the mirror hanging above the sink. The goose egg nesting on the top corner of her forehead stood out like a beacon. She had to be suffering from a concussion. Why else would she be acting this way?

It was her desperate attempt to make sense of it all. She examined the rest of her reflection and her overall disheveled appearance. She looked like something the cat dragged in, quite different from her handsome rescuer, who looked like a *Men's Health* magazine model. Her mind freely wandered across every square inch of his perfect torso, starting at the wide expanse of his muscular shoulders and down the flat plane of his stomach.

"Raine?"

Patrick's voice interrupted her thoughts. "Um…yeah?"

"Are you sure you're all right? You're spacing out constantly, and that's not like you. Ever since you hit your head, you've been acting strange."

Patrick's words convinced her even more. "You're right. I think I just need to rest."

"Or better yet, see a doctor. They actually have those in Ireland too, you know."

Lorraine remembered the man mentioning a doctor up the road. "I was told there was a doctor up the street. I'll look into it tomorrow."

As she disconnected the call, she took one last look in the mirror. What she wouldn't give to have a shower right now, but that was asking too much. Her host had already done enough for her. Between getting caught in a storm and babysitting, she'd caused him enough inconvenience as it was. It was best she leave.

She gathered up the change of clothes he generously offered her and slung her backpack over her shoulder. Her only thoughts were on making an escape without looking any more ridiculous than before.

Taking a deep breath, she unlocked the door and burst through. A brick wall of solid male chest stopped her. She looked up, stunned.

He looked her over. "You didn't change?"

"I know. I decided there was no sense in it. I'd only get your clothes wet when I hike back to my B&B."

"You're not hiking anywhere. Especially not in this storm."

"I realize it's raining, but this is Ireland, and I've come dressed for the occasion." She tugged on the collar of her raincoat and aimed to step forward.

He crossed his arms and leaned against the frame of the door, blocking her in. "I don't think so, love. If I let you leave, it would tarnish my honor."

"Your...*honor*?"

"Indeed. To let a poor, injured beauty like yourself wander the craggy fields of Erin in a terrible storm...well, that wouldn't be very noble of me, now would it? Besides, I have enough fish searing in the kitchen for two. Hungry?"

Starving. But all she really heard was a "beauty like yourself." Did he really think that or was he just being charming? She glanced over her appearance. *Don't flatter yourself, Raine.* "I appreciate all that you've done for me, but I really must go." She tried to sneak past him again, but he didn't budge. In fact, he stepped toward her, forcing her to take a few steps backward. His virile male scent surrounded her, and she recognized it as if she'd drawn it in many times before.

"Look," he explained. "I think you and I got off on the wrong foot. Somewhere between you falling on your face and you waking up in my home, a much-needed pleasantry has been overlooked. How about we start over? Say with introductions?" With a casual grace, he reached into the small closet door to the right and pulled out a fluffy white towel. Handing it forward, he smiled. "My name is Leif. Leif Dæganssen. I'm an archeologist from—"

"Hladir?"

His eyes lit up, and Lorraine covered her mouth. She had no idea where Hladir was, but for some reason after hearing his last name, the place name just came out.

Leif cocked his head. "Hladir hasn't existed since the eleventh century, but its location is in the vicinity of Trondheim, which is where I'm originally from. How did you know that? Are you a historian or something?"

How did I know that? She stumbled again on her words, loathing the fact that every time she spoke to him, she sounded like a babbling idiot. "L-lucky guess?" He didn't buy it. "Really, I have no idea where that came from." She squeezed her eyes shut. "Right now, I have no idea where anything is coming from. I swear to you, I'm not crazy. I'm just a small-town Kentucky girl who feels about as lost as a needle in a haystack."

He held her by the arms now, gripping gently above her elbows. "It's all right. You don't have to explain. I've seen my share of head injuries from collapsing castle ruins. It's obvious you have a concussion, and we'll get you to a doctor in the morning. So for now, it's best you stay put. I know you're wary of spending the night in a stranger's home, but there's nothing the Man of Aran Cottage has to offer that I can't. I have a spare room, complete with a working lock," he added with wink. "I have a fireplace, hot running water, and a complimentary meal ready for the eating. I can't promise the food is as good as Maura Wolfe's, but it's edible. So, what's it to be?"

Did she actually have a choice? And how could she possibly turn him down? Everything sounded inviting, especially the hot shower and food. Reluctantly, she accepted his offer, though she could hear Patrick's rebuttal all the way from the States.

Leif flashed a smile, revealing a set of perfect white teeth, parenthesized by deep, endearing laugh lines. "I'll leave you to your shower, then." Bending slightly at the waist, as if in a noble bow, he backed out of the bathroom.

"I'm Raine," she spat hastily.

He froze at the door, and his eyes pierced her soul. "You're what?"

"I mean, my name is Lorraine O'Connor. But my friends call me Raine."

Another dazzling smile crossed his lips. "Then Raine it is."

He held her gaze for some time, as if he were turning her name over in his mind, testing the sound of it. She liked the sound of his name as well. It was distinctive, strong, and oh so Norse. It fit him well.

"Holler if you need anything else."

As he closed the door, she stepped forward and leaned against it. Everything about Leif was kind and alluring: his deep resonating voice, his husky scent, and his mesmerizing eyes. But then she heard the echo of Patrick's voice warning her, and for no other reason than to satisfy him, she reached down and turned the lock.

Chapter Six

Leif laughed inwardly as he heard the lock engage. Lorraine was definitely an odd sort of female with all her outlandish outbursts and peculiar reactions, but no less interesting. She had a way about her that made him pay close attention. Made him *want* to pay close attention, else he might miss something. No woman had ever been able to do that to him.

He was not a man easily beguiled. "Exceedingly picky" were Kristoff's words on many occasions when they could've had a few choice opportunities with several of the women who entered Tí Joe Mac's Pub in Kilronan. But he always found a way to stay clear. Either their hair was too short, their fingers too long, or they were excessively giggly over anyone who spoke Gaelic to them. No matter how beautiful they were, Leif always managed to find a flaw he couldn't get past.

The only imperfection Lorraine possessed was being unreadable. Even then, he couldn't rightfully hold it against her. He was glad she left him guessing, left him wondering what she'd say or do next. Every time he spoke to her, he had no idea what would come out of her mouth.

And what a pretty mouth it is.

Her lips were a delicate shade of rose and looked just as supple as the petals from which its color derived. He imagined they felt as soft and delicate in a kiss.

And then there were her eyes. They shone as bright as

the intrinsic color of an emerald, with flecks of lighter green pigments fissuring throughout. Though they resembled rare jewels, he couldn't help but feel he'd admired them before. Words couldn't describe what he felt, except that his longing was innate—as if her eyes and all their wonders had been engraved on him from years past.

Again, he laughed, reminding himself that his entire week had been absurd. Between finding the carved chest buried beside his porch, to having a gorgeous woman drop out of thin air at his feet, he could hardly believe his bizarre stroke of luck.

He strolled back to the kitchen and set the table for dinner, his thoughts still centered on Raine. By the time he finished pouring their drinks, he smelled charred seafood and dashed toward the stove to flip the fish in the pan. He'd been so distracted that he almost burned the meal he'd promised her. At least he was still a red-blooded man with working parts. As many times as Kristoff had ridiculed him for his lack of interest in women, he'd almost begun to worry. Raine proved otherwise, as she definitely roused more than his curiosity.

"It smells delicious."

Leif started at the sound of Lorraine's voice and almost knocked the pan off the stove. Fortunately, he caught it by the handle and steadied it before it toppled off the edge.

"I take it you're not used to a woman in your home," she said.

He heaved a sigh rather than try to explain why he'd suddenly jumped. "How was your shower?"

"Exhilarating. Thank you."

He turned back to the fish simmering on the stove and rallied his best casual voice. "Good. Glad to hear that." As he resumed cooking, he brought to mind how great she looked in his T-shirt. Just knowing that his clothes enveloped every curve of her body had him thinking that he'd never been so jealous. What's more, he might never wash that shirt again.

"Since my clothes were still damp, I hung them over the shower rod to dry," she confessed. "I hope that's all right."

His grip tightened on the handle of the pan. The image of a lacey bra and delicate panties dangling in his bathroom flashed in his mind. Crueler still, he realized she was likely going commando beneath his clothes. Without facing her, he shrugged and fisted a quartered lemon above the pan-seared cod, dousing it with lemon juice. "Sure. That's fine. I hope you're hungry. I've made enough for the whole village."

He thought he heard a slight chuckle, regretting that he'd probably missed the first opportunity to see her smile. But he kept to his mission of transferring the food to the two plates sitting on the adjacent counter. It required more of his attention given he wasn't a practiced chef.

He added the final touches to the plate with a few island flowers he'd picked days ago—only because he heard from the more experienced chefs in Dublin's pricey restaurants that presentation was everything—and a slice of soda bread on top. He turned around and caught her looking at him, but she quickly cleared her throat and averted her gaze. For her sake, he acted as if he hadn't noticed. "Please. Have a seat."

She did as he suggested, wringing her hands in the extra length of T-shirt. He sat opposite her at the table instead of sharing the same corner since she still seemed nervous. At present, she sat stiff-backed in the chair, her eyes fixed on the bounty of food he placed in front of her.

She smiled when she saw the white-and-yellow daisy garnishing her plate. She never said a word about the embellishment, but her pleasant expression was enough.

He watched her take the first bite. Her eyes closed as she pulled the fork from her mouth and her shoulders melted.

"Does that mean it's good?" he asked.

"Are you kidding? This is the best pan-seared fish I've ever had."

"Now I'm convinced you have a concussion."

"I'm serious. I've never had fish like this before. Most times it's fried to a crisp or bland as hell."

"Well, I don't know much about Kentucky, but I believe it's known for its horses, not herbs." He took his first bite and waited. "What? That wasn't funny?"

She stuffed a piece of bread in her mouth as though to hide a grin. "You make a better cook than a comedian."

"Ah, look at that. Give the small-town Kentucky girl a hot shower and some food and she's as good as new."

"I don't know about all that," she replied, dabbing the corner of her mouth with her napkin.

"Well, you're gaining a bit of confidence. It's good to know you're less fearful of me."

Her hand froze at her lips. "I don't fear you, Leif. I just don't know you."

He set his utensil down and crossed his arms, eager to finally delve into a meaningful discussion. "What is it you'd like to know?"

I shied from his intrusive eyes, the heat of his stare setting me ablaze.

"I know you're avoiding me because you feel 'tis right. 'Tis moral. 'Tis safer. But you needn't fear me."

I took a deep breath. "I do not fear you, Dægan. I simply do not know enough about you."

He drew back his face as if my choice of words stunned him. He released me and crossed his arms. "What would you like to know?"

"Raine?"

Leif's voice caught her off guard, and the name *Dægan* echoed in her ears. She blinked, staring at the man whose face showed as much confusion as hers must.

"Lorraine, are you all right?" he asked again, reaching across the table for her hand.

Instantly, she pulled away and tried to gather her wits. It seemed she'd heard Leif's words and the same words from a man named Dægan simultaneously. What the hell was wrong with her? Why did she keep seeing things that weren't really there? Or hear conversations from someone's past that were so akin to what she was talking about now?

"You blacked out for a moment," Leif explained.

"I did?" The question came out even though she knew she'd gone somewhere else. Somewhere that seemed like a memory, as though she were having a personal recollection of long ago between her and a Norse warrior.

"Yeah, you did. I asked you what you wanted to know about me, and suddenly, your eyes glazed over. You stared straight forward but focused on nothing. Are you sure you're all right? It might be best to call the doctor right now."

She fidgeted in her chair. The thought of a doctor looking her over and determining she was categorically crazy was not in her vacation plans. She tried to go back to her normal routine of eating and talking to prove to him that he was overreacting. "Really, I'm fine. You shouldn't worry. I just need to finish eating and get some rest. I've had a long day."

Again, he didn't look convinced, but what else could she say? That was the only rational explanation for what was happening to her.

During the rest of the meal, they ate without making any more small talk. The only sound heard was the casual clinking of silverware. Despite the great food and warm hospitality, Lorraine wanted nothing more than to lie down and sleep this off, whatever it was.

Chapter Seven

Leif's spare bedroom was quaint and simple in its decorations, with a single window on the far wall. The curtains were plain white cotton, which matched the duvet on the queen-size bed centered in the room. Above that hung a picture of a long-haired medieval maiden in a small boat with her embroidered tapestry hanging over the side, a classic John William Waterhouse painting in a fanciful, carved frame.

"Isn't that *The Lady of Shalott*?" Lorraine asked.

"What can I say? I'm a romantic."

If she could say anything about Leif, he was certainly a one-of-a-kind gentleman. How often did a woman find herself carried off by a handsome man on horseback who cooked and was into sappy nineteenth century Renaissance art?

His arm brushed against hers as he moved toward the dresser. "There's extra blankets in here, in case you get cold. And there's an alarm clock on the table if you want to get up early. The sun rises at four a.m., which..." he looked at his watch, "...is about six hours from now."

Lorraine rocked back and forth on her heels. "I'm not much of an early riser. I think I'll pass on the alarm."

"Fair enough," he said, smiling. "Then I won't wake you."

As soon as she thought he'd leave the room, he surprised her and leaned against the dresser, crossing his ankles. "I'm going to go out on a limb here, so you'll have to excuse me if I sound stereotypical, but I assume that since you're from Kentucky, you know your way around horses, right?"

"I know enough. Why?"

"Well, I thought I'd offer to give you a tour of Inishmore…on horseback…if you'd like. It beats touring the island on a bike."

She was certain it did but hadn't expected him to offer such a thing. "Are you sure you want to do that?"

His expression fell toward disappointed. "Why wouldn't I?"

"I don't know. I just figured you'd be counting the hours to when I'd leave."

Leif pushed himself from the dresser and approached her. Each step he took jolted her heart to new heights. He might have been aloof all evening, but now his cobalt eyes held her gaze with such intensity that there was no chance of turning away.

He stopped inches from her without touching. His gaze fell to her lips, then back to her eyes. "You're welcome to stay as long as you like." After that, he cleared the huskiness from his throat, uttered a kind farewell, and left.

Lorraine finally breathed the moment she heard the door close behind her. She wasn't quite sure how she managed to stay standing given her legs felt as wobbly as a newborn foal's.

She hurried over to the bed and sat down. As tame and poised as Leif seemed to be, she also sensed he had a wild streak. There was an unrestrained fierceness to his nature, and she wasn't used to that level of rugged virility. Neither Patrick nor Brad possessed such dominant qualities, but she didn't mind the differences either.

He seems almost too good to be true.

She could hear Patrick saying the same thing, warning her against Leif's invitation to tour the island with him. *"Raine, you're on the rebound. This trip was to get away from men, not lure another one in."*

She flopped back on the bed and stared at the wooden beams above her. As much as she hated listening to reason, she knew it was her best friend right now. She didn't need to get involved with a man on her vacation. It defeated the point of the trip, and most likely she'd only set herself up for another heartache.

Even if Leif was her knight in shining armor, she lived in Kentucky and he in Ireland. Long-distance relationships never worked, and she sure as hell couldn't see him packing up his life or his work just to jet off with her to the States. He was a European archeologist who probably had no interest in digging up arrowheads and Civil War musket balls. At least in the British Isles, where history spanned as far back as the Bronze Age, there were more opportunities and larger prospects for ancient digs. Leif would be foolish to follow her to the newborn States.

Lorraine furrowed her brow. How could she lie there and devise excuses as to why Leif shouldn't tag along with her to Kentucky when they weren't in a relationship to begin with? Not even a hint of one. Sure, they seemed to have a rapport with each other, but then again, she also had a rapport with her parish priest.

Oh, dear God.

She *had* to have a concussion. With as many off-the-wall thoughts as she'd had today, there was no denying it. All she needed was a good night's sleep and a fresh start in the morning.

She dragged herself up to the head of the bed and snuggled deep beneath the covers, only to be surrounded by the scent of Leif's laundry detergent, which again reminded her of him.

Blissful sleep was but a deep breath away.

****

Leif entered his own bedroom and closed the door, unable to contain his amusement. He could still see the way Lorraine stiffened when he drew close, and the hint of lust in her eyes after he spoke to her.

He probably shouldn't have encouraged her to stay with such a raspy, flirtatious tone given the apprehension she felt in staying the night in his home. But it just came out that way. And as crazy as it sounded, he meant it. He wanted to know more about her. Why she'd come to Ireland. Why she'd come alone. What she did for a living. What her favorite flower was. Everything. Nothing was too trivial. He wanted to know every detail about Lorraine O'Connor.

Chapter Eight

Lorraine threw the warm covers off her body in frustration. It was the worst sleep she'd ever had, bouncing back and forth between sweet dreams and vivid nightmares. On some occasions, Leif—or rather, the handsome Viking warrior who looked like Leif—had held her close with loving tenderness and kissed her. But at other moments, he'd manhandle her to the ground and pin her there. It was the most exasperating feeling to swing like a pendulum between the two with no rhyme or reason. And now that it was ten a.m. with the bright sun blazing through the thin white curtains, she knew there was no hope of finding any kind of sound sleep at all.

Leif was both a curse and cure. While he plagued her with an assortment of emotions she couldn't fully grasp, he was therapy for making her forget all about her breakup with Brad. From the time she'd laid eyes on Leif sitting magnificently on his horse, she'd never thought of Brad once.

Smiling from that revelation, she sat up, stretched, and decided to see if Leif was awake. As she padded across the cool hardwood floor, she remembered what he'd said to her: *"You're welcome to stay as long as you like."*

It wasn't necessarily what he said, but how he said it. He delivered it with heat and seduction while eyeing her mouth. If only he knew the heavy influx of emotions he'd caused her with that little trick.

She flung open the door and found a pile of neatly folded clothes at her feet—her clothes, washed and dried—with a note on top. She retrieved the letter and the sight of his handwritten script made her even giddier than knowing he did her laundry.

Not ready to wash my hands of you yet, but I did wash your clothes.
Leif
PS, I'm in the barn

****

Kristoff leaned against the wall and watched Leif brush down a pair of horses, each in their own stall. "I see you've finally found someone to go riding with you."

The woman he'd met last night brought more excitement in one short evening than he'd had in all his life. Even the upsurge of emotions he'd felt seven years ago when he and a team of archeologists discovered a rare Viking grave of a prominent warrior in Waterford didn't come close.

"Am I ever going to get to meet her?" Kristoff probed.

Leif looked up from his grooming and tossed the brush, currycomb, and hoof pick to Kristoff. He knew all too well that his brother usually had his own agenda when it came to women, and the fact that Leif might already have an interest in one didn't seem to deter him. "Depends on your intention, and what you mean by 'meet.'"

"Meet. Say hello, my name is…"

Leif stepped out of the stall momentarily to grab the pad and saddle from the rack on the wall, then stepped back in to throw it up on his horse's back. He hardly bought a word of Kristoff's blasé clarification. "Perhaps you'll meet her when I'm good and ready to let you."

Kristoff laughed aloud and juggled the grooming tools in a graceful arc. "At least tell me what her name is."

Leif sighed. "Her name is Lorraine. And that's all you need to know."

"You're worried she'll choose me over you."

"You'd like to think that, wouldn't you? But no. I'm more worried you'll make a bad impression."

Kristoff caught the brushes in midair and smiled. "You like her, don't you?"

Leif grunted as he tightened the girth. "I already told you I did. Now, make yourself useful and hand me Thor's bridle."

Kristoff reached around the tack door to his right and lifted the leather headstall from the hook. "This one?"

Leif snatched it from his brother's hands, wondering how a man who'd made his living hauling tourists around in horse-drawn carriages couldn't remember which head harness went with which horse. "Yes, that one."

As Leif slipped the bit into Thor's mouth and pulled the headpiece over his ears, his thoughts somehow ran back to Lorraine. He decided if she hadn't made an appearance by the time he finished tacking up the horses, he'd have to check on her. As much as he hated to barge into her private room, he wondered if she'd ditched his clothes and slept naked.

Yep, I'm a man. And a pig too, it seems.

He then exited Thor's stall, stole the currycombs from his brother's hands, and entered Freyja's stall to do the same. He made fast work of brushing her down and picking her hooves.

"On a mission, I see," Kristoff said. "Well, since you've obviously laid claim to Laurel, how 'bout you introduce me to one of the friends she's vacationing with?"

"Her name is Lorraine, and you're shit out of luck. She came to Ireland by herself."

"Are you kidding me?"

"Nope."

"Who the hell ventures off to another country alone? I mean, that makes about as much sense as you naming your nags after Norse gods."

Leif straightened from brushing Freyja's belly. "Don't call my horses nags. And if you had any balls at all, you'd ditch the carriage and ride Thor like a real man—on his back. Then you'd know he's rightfully named."

"Why? So I can hear the thunder of his hooves?" Kristoff taunted as he caught the grooming tools Leif threw at him again. "Believe me, the good Lord didn't give me a set of balls so I could feel a horse beneath me."

Leif actually laughed at his brother's joke. "I guess I can't argue with you there." He thought he'd ended the conversation, but Kristoff continued to pry.

"So, where are you taking her today?"

Leif fetched Freyja's saddle and righted it behind her withers, wishing his brother had better things to do. "Don't you have some honeymooning tourists who need to get to the ferry in a few hours?"

"I see how you are. Dismissing me. Just like you did the other night."

"I'm going to assume you're referring to the night we found the chest."

"I figured you would've done something with it by now instead of letting it gather dust in your bedroom.

Especially since you're so passionate about finding who your ancestors are."

Leif secured the girth, then patted Freyja's rump as he understood Kristoff's implication. "I know what you would like me to do with it, and I can appreciate that. But this chest is not about fame or fortune."

"You're sitting on a gold mine, Leif, and you expect me to turn my back on that. Wouldn't you like to see your name credited with an incredible find instead of just being on the team of unmentioned diggers? Seriously, this is huge. Confirmed Viking graves are rare in Ireland."

"I'm well aware of that," Leif said calmly. "But I don't think we stumbled onto a gravesite. Where's the sword? A shield boss? Coins or bone combs? There was nothing of the sort buried with it."

"It was storming and near midnight when we unearthed that chest. We couldn't see the broadside of a longship if we wanted to that night. Your entire house could be sitting on a warrior's gravesite for all we know, just waiting to be discovered, and yet you're content to do nothing."

"You may think I've done nothing, but while you've been gallivanting with female tourists at the pubs every night, I made a trip to Dublin a few days ago and used my credentials to score access to the original manuscript of the *Annals of Ulster* in Trinity's library."

Kristoff held his emotions in check. "Go on..."

"In that document, it dictates countless historical events about the Norse invasions in Ireland, particularly the Irish chieftains who attempted to unite and banish them from their lands."

"So, what does this have to do with the chest?"

"I found a snippet of text suggesting that one king refused to join the campaign. It doesn't give specifics, but there is mention of a truce offering between him and an unknown heathen foreigner."

"And you're thinking the chest might be…"

"I've no idea. I'd like to believe I've unearthed their little token of peace, but until the carbon data comes back from the lab, it's all speculation. My gut tells me there's greater significance with the chest than just an allegorical peace offering. Unfortunately, any trace of a legendary chest dating back to that era is miniscule at best. There's little to no evidence one even exists."

Kristoff planted his hands on his hips. "And you quit there? You're so close," he exclaimed. "You could have evidence proving that the Norse who inhabited this isle were not here through forceful means, but by treaty."

Kristoff was right. He could be sitting on an extraordinary historical find, one that could change the views of historians and history books forever. It could very well help prove his ancestors had arrived and settled the harsh Aran Islands because both parties sought an alliance and continued to live with the Gaels for hundreds of years before the Viking Era died out. He was even eager to conduct a thorough clandestine dig beneath the crawl space of his cottage, but since Lorraine had fallen into his world, she'd sharply diverted his attention. Surely Kristoff and his overactive libido could appreciate that.

"Look," Leif defended, keeping his voice low. "I have every intention of continuing my research. But right now, it's come to a screeching halt."

"Oooooh, screeching halt. That sounds interesting. What would that be?"

Both men froze at the sound of a female's voice

behind them.

As Lorraine entered the spacious barn, she inhaled the familiar scent of weathered wood, leather, and horse. It smelled like Patrick's barn, and she welcomed the distinct, countrified aroma of home.

She glanced between Leif in the stalls and the man he was conversing with. He stood as tall as Leif, with a day-old shadow of a beard across his face, and just as handsome. His jeans fit snuggly around his thighs, and by the wry grin that twitched at his mouth, she assumed he wore them more for a woman's pleasure than his own comfort.

Judging by their lack of response, she detected that she'd probably walked in on a private conversation. After a few moments of awkward silence, the man in the overly tight jeans spoke first.

"If you must know," he offered smoothly. "Leif's birthday celebration has come to a screeching halt."

Lorraine watched as the two exchanged peculiar looks. When Leif didn't offer the backup the man seemed to be fishing for, he finally ventured out on his own.

"It was supposed to be this Friday at Tí Joe Watty's Bar, but since he's entertaining a guest now, we could always move it to a later date."

Lorraine cocked her head. "Why would you do that?"

The man shuffled his feet. "Because…your time in Ireland is limited. I'm sure your itinerary didn't include drinking Guinness with a couple of Norwegians."

Lorraine smiled, gazing deeply into Leif's eyes. "Sounds like fun. I might be able to work that into my tight schedule of tourist attractions."

"Well, there we go," the man said, slapping his hands together and rubbing them. "The party resumes."

Leif furrowed his brow. "I suppose it does."

"I'm Kristoff, by the way. Leif's brother." He tucked the horse combs under his left arm and offered his other hand in a shake.

Incredulous of the explanation Kristoff gave, she shook his hand anyway. "AKA partner in crime?"

Kristoff let out a short laugh. "Ah, looks like my reputation has preceded me once again."

"Something tells me you prefer it that way."

Leif lowered his gaze to the ground as if trying to keep his laughter from erupting. Kristoff noticed it too. "I guess that was my cue to head on out," Kristoff said, thumbing toward the outside of the barn.

"Yeah, genius, I think it was," Leif jeered, leaning against his horse.

Lorraine felt guilty. "I'm sorry, I didn't mean it like that."

"Trust me, Raine," Leif cajoled as he stroked the horse's muzzle. "You won't want Kristoff to stick around any longer than he has to."

"He's right," Kristoff agreed, backing out the aisleway. "I'm boring as hell, I have two left feet, and I have this terrible habit of pleasing every woman who graces my bed. I ruin her for every other man she meets. It's a curse of mine. Truly, it is."

"You're also cursed with your head stuck up your arse." Leif waved his fingers in a gimme gesture. "My currycombs?"

Kristoff tossed the brushes to Lorraine. "Friday, then. Seven. You better be there."

Lorraine exchanged looks with Leif while running her

palm over the soft bristles. "I wouldn't miss it."

Chapter Nine

Lorraine took a deep breath as the silence between her and Leif lengthened. "I didn't mean to berate your brother," she said, inching closer to the stall gate that separated them. "Sometimes my snarky behavior gets the best of me."

"No need to apologize. I enjoyed every blessed minute of it. Not many women can put Kristoff in his place." He secured the throatlatch on Freyja's bridle and led her out of the stall. "Are you still ready to go on that ride with me?"

"Of course. Is this my horse for the day?"

"Indeed. Her name's Freyja."

"Isn't that the name of a Norse goddess? Goddess of passion, love, and fertility?"

"Impressive."

"Freshman English lit teacher. He was a big fan of mythology." Lorraine looked the horse over. "She's beautiful."

Leif watched as she reached out and petted the horse's muzzle. As her dainty fingers ran smoothly over Freyja's forehead, he was now envious of his mare. He wished he too could feel the soft stroke of her hand along his body. He didn't care where. At this point, he'd take an innocent caress across his own forehead if it suited her.

Steering his thoughts to things that might actually happen, he spoke of their plans for the day. "Are you hungry? I figured after we pay the doctor a visit, I'll take you to Tí Joe Watty's, and you can taste those famous fish 'n' chips I told you about—if you're not opposed to eating lunch for breakfast."

"I can eat anything, no matter what time of day it is," she confessed. "But really, I'm fine. We don't have to bother the doctor."

"It's not a bother. I promised you, and that's what we're doing."

"Seriously, there's no need. I'm much better now."

Leif's inner voice argued against her. "And what if you get hurt on this horse today because your wits are still jumbled? I'd never forgive myself."

"My wits are fine," she stated. "Test me if you don't believe me."

Leif's mouth twitched in a grin, partially because of the way she dared him. "All right," he muttered, taking a step closer. "What day is it?" He brushed back a strand of her hair and let his fingers caress the rim of her ear before he traced her jaw and lifted her chin. To his surprise, she rattled off her answer with no hesitation.

"It's Wednesday, June fifteenth, which means I have less than two days to figure out what I'm giving you for your birthday, if, in fact, the seventeenth is really the date of your birth."

Leif gazed into her eyes, taking in their clarity and the responsiveness of her pupils. He hardly thought he could be as poised if she'd done the same to him. "Well done, but I'm still keeping an eye on you. One slipup and I'm dragging you to Dr. O'Donnell's residence. By your hair, if I have to. Understand?"

"Understood."

Leif liked her a lot. Everything about her, her green

eyes, her sweet scent, her feisty façade…every little thing enticed him to be brazen and bold. Ignoring the temptation to haul her over his shoulder to the doctor's anyway, he led Thor out of his stall and mounted.

"For someone who's supposed to have their wits about them," Lorraine began to say as she also hoisted herself in the saddle, "yours aren't so sharp either."

Leif eyed her curiously. "What do you mean?"

She adjusted herself in the saddle and tested her stirrup lengths by standing in them. "You never answered me."

"I don't recall you ever asking me a question."

"Technically, I didn't. But I did make a statement that warranted a response. Is your birthday really on the seventeenth, or is that just the day of the celebration?"

A slight chuckle escaped him as he tightened up on his reins and held his anxious horse at bay. "My birthday is not the seventeenth. And no gifts are necessary."

Lorraine clicked her tongue and urged her horse forward with Leif mirroring her pace. "Do I get to know the date of your birth?"

"That knowledge is usually saved for my closest friends, so we'll see how the day goes."

She grinned in a way that would light up the darkest night. "How am I doing so far?"

Leif returned the smile as he looked up to the sky, hoping the weather would cooperate with the plans he'd made. "Splendidly."

She shrugged as if mildly impressed. "Fortunately for you, I'm willing to forgive your joke about dragging me by the hair."

He reached across and gently took hold of her left hand, lifting it out of respect. He locked eyes with her and bowed slightly. "I *am* fortunate."

Lorraine's stomach twisted into knots as she felt the solid warmth of his hand beneath her palm and the strength of his fingers. She blinked rapidly through the gesture and drew in a slow, steady breath, trying to settle her racing heart. She had to get ahold of herself. Fainting, falling flat on her face, and talking out of her head wasn't the kind of behavior that attracted a man like Leif. He was a self-assured, physically fit, intelligent male who had better things to do with his time than waste it on a woman who couldn't keep it together.

"You're awfully quiet," Leif said, jolting her back to reality. "Did I say something wrong?"

She waved him off. "I think I'm just hungry."

Leif raised his finger, indicating he had something for her. He unzipped his cantle bag behind him and pulled out a granola bar. "Here, this should hold you until we get to Joe's. Unless you'd like something else?"

"No, this is fine. Thank you." She glanced back at his open, overstuffed pouch, seeing a few things that were not the normal saddlebag items. "What else you do have in there?"

He zipped it back up. "That's for later."

"Did I see seriously just see a can of whipped cream?"

"I'm not saying anything more, so quit asking."

Lorraine couldn't contain her curiosity. What kind of horseman packed whipping cream in his saddle bag? It was definitely not the typical item found on the list of what smart riders pack in case of emergencies. Flashlights, beef jerky, leather, and a log of Duraflame Firestart—those were essentials. Whipped cream was for apple pies, sundaes, and lovers trying to spice up their relationship. They weren't lovers, and Leif didn't seem like the type of guy who needed condiments to liven things up or, rather, any help in that department at all.

She peeled the granola bar open and took a bite, trying to give her roaming thoughts a rest.

"What do you do for a living, Raine?"

His question caught her off guard, and she purposefully took longer to chew and swallow in order to bide some time. Leif was an archeologist. She was a bartender. Not exactly the career she dreamed of, but considering the short amount of hours she put in weekly, she made damn good money. "I work at an Irish pub back in the States. I tend bar."

"Really."

"I know, it's not the best career choice I could've made for myself, but the owners are like family to me."

"Do you enjoy it?"

Lorraine thought back to the busy nights she had spent at Molly Malone's, sliding pint glass after pint glass of Guinness and Irish Car Bombs across the lacquered bar to enthusiastic Reds and Bengals fans after a game-day win. Or the slower nights when she'd lend an ear to one of the regulars who was going through a layoff at Procter & Gamble. And who could forget the crowds of Irish wannabees on St. Patrick's Day?

Yeah, she loved it. It wasn't about serving drinks. It was about being there for customers when they needed someone. Sometimes patrons came in to celebrate a new birth in the family or the graduation of a son who'd surpassed everyone's expectations in college. Other times it was to grieve over the loss of a loved one, or the final signing of divorce papers. No matter what the reason, they came to that establishment for support, and she enjoyed being needed.

Needed.

Brad didn't need her. He never had, come to think of it. Maybe that was why she clung to the bar so tightly. It was the one place she felt in control and important despite the many arguments it started, because he wanted her to quit and go back to college. *"Get a job you can be proud of,"* he'd say.

"Yeah, I do like it," she affirmed.

"Then, that's all that matters. It sure beats having a PhD behind your name and hating every minute of it."

"I guess so."

"You don't believe me?"

"No, I believe you," she said, taking another bite and wishing he'd let it go.

"Let me guess, someone doesn't approve of your occupation."

"You could say that." She shrugged. "But I don't care what he thinks."

Silence lengthened between them, and the only sound was the slow cadence of rhythmic hoofbeats on the paved road. She thought he'd given up, happy that he might have, and looked out into the distance over the pattern of rock-walled pastures while she rocked in the saddle.

"Would this person," he inquired, much to her disappointment, "whose thoughts you couldn't care less about happen to be your boyfriend?"

"I don't have a boyfriend."

"I sense some animosity," he prodded further. "How long has it been?"

She gave him a sideways glance. "How long has what

been?"

"Since you found out your boyfriend was unfaithful."

Choking on the last bite of her snack, she milked the time it took to cough it clear. How did he know that? Was she that easy to read? Or was he an accomplished mind reader?

By the time she was ready to face him and explain, he was holding out an ice-cold water bottle. She gratefully took what he had to offer, uncapped it, and drank heavily, her mind frazzled.

She lowered the bottle, eyeing the sweat on the side to give her something to look at other than Leif. The last thing she wanted to do was bring her troubles along with her to Ireland. She was perfectly content to leave them behind. The whole purpose of this vacation had been to forget about Brad and his infidelity. Now that she found a man worthy of making her forget, she sure as heck didn't want to make him think he was the rebound guy. That said, she wasn't a good liar either.

"I found out that he'd been unfaithful...a few days ago."

As soon as the words came out of her mouth, she regretted them. She knew whatever chance she had with Leif had now been dimmed. Or worse—destroyed. She couldn't look at him, or bear to see the vivid storms of blue in his eyes paling to a mediocre color of disappointment. She took another drink. The second bout of awkward silence raked on her nerves like nails down a chalkboard.

"Raine." His deep voice washed over her like silk. "Is that why you're here? Alone?"

Oh, it sounded so pitiful coming from him. "Yes."

Embarrassment burned in her cheeks, and she wished she could suddenly disappear. She didn't want to drag this day out any longer than necessary. He was clearly ready to move on from her now, and she wouldn't be surprised if he decided to end his horse-guided tour of Inishmore prematurely. She had entirely too much baggage for one man to handle.

"Raine?"

Eyes front, she kept her horse walking.

"Raine?" he repeated, halting his horse abruptly.

Hers did the same, and she prepared herself for a gentle letdown. He reined his horse one-eighty so he faced her. Their knees bumped, and he took hold of her chin, lifting her eyes to meet his gaze. "It's his loss…and my gain."

Chapter Ten

Leif's words took her by complete surprise. If he hadn't had a hold of her, she probably would've fallen backward off her horse. She stared at him, wondering if she heard him correctly. Or maybe this was another episode of imagining things that weren't really happening.

"Raine, you have about five seconds to say something halfway intelligible before I haul you over my shoulder to Doctor O'Donnell's."

Her heart sped up as she glanced at his lips, full, perfect, and parted, waiting for her to respond. He looked at her lips too, and the moments ticked by between them. It almost felt as if he were about to kiss her should she say the right thing. The hunger in his eyes seemed insatiable at best, and nothing came to mind except for the thought of her own hunger for him.

"I'm hungry," she mumbled.

Hearty laughter erupted from him. "Intelligible enough, I suppose. Not what I predicted, but it was, indeed, intelligible. If we pick up the pace, I imagine we can have you fed in less than ten minutes." He tilted his head in a delicate dare. "Are you game?"

Lorraine was not so disoriented as to miss his subtle challenge. She fed on dares, especially those that involved sprinting horses. She shook away the evocative cobwebs of his touch and his voice, then gathered her reins and pushed against her stirrups, heels down, preparing to bolt at his say-so.

"I take it that's a—"

Lorraine drove her heels into Freyja's flank, and the mare lunged forward, leaving Leif in the dust.

****

"For the winner," Leif declared, setting the Catch of the Day with Chips in front of Lorraine on the outdoor picnic table at Joe Watty's bar. "Remember, we have to eat fast. With the horses hobbled, I'm not so worried about them walking away as much as I'm fretting dung cleanup."

Her eyes were as big as pint rims as she stared at the heaping plate. "Um…surely this isn't all for me?"

He took a huge gulp of his Guinness and settled in across from her. "What you can't eat, I'll finish." It was cute how she raised her brow and folded her hands in her lap as if contemplating where to start.

"I could use your help now."

Leif sat up and leaned forward, snatching a narrow plank of fish and holding it to her lips.

Lorraine glanced at the food and back at him. "What are you doing?"

"Helping you eat."

"I didn't mean help me like that. I meant for you to eat some *with* me."

Leif kept the battered fish hovering at lip level. "Come on, humor me."

Lorraine shifted her eyes across the many picnic tables crowded with camera-toting, raincoat-wearing tourists. "Here? In this place?"

"Sure. Why not?"

"Because it's a public place. People will see."

"It's a pub," he reminded her. "I think they've seen far worse things than a woman eating from a man's hand. Hell, I think last week they found a couple passed out on this very table—in position."

Lorraine's eyes widened even more. "In position like...*that* kind of position? You're kidding."

"Actually, I am." Ducking, he dodged a chip she snatched from her plate. "You'll throw food in a public place but you won't eat from my hand?"

"All right, if it'll make you happy."

He half expected her to take a quick bite, over and done with before he could get a chance to relish her open mouth. But she proved him wrong.

She placed her hand on his, steadying him, and slowly parted her lips. Guiding the plank into her mouth, she closed her lips around his fingertips and sank her teeth into the flesh of the fish, pulling away. Her little pink tongue darted out and licked the tiny particles of batter left on her bottom lip.

Leif about fell over.

His limbs went numb, and all the blood plummeted from his brain to his groin. He couldn't think. He couldn't speak. What does a man say after a sight like that?

He asked for it, so he couldn't say he didn't know it was coming. But he sure as heck wasn't prepared to see her accommodate his wishes with such allure. He rocked in his seat and rubbed his scruffy jaw, but it did nothing to alleviate his raging imagination.

"You gonna be all right there, Leif? I know a good doctor down the road."

He tried laughing it off. When that didn't help, he scooped up his pint glass and guzzled the beer. "You're right," he muttered, slamming his glass to the table. "A woman should never eat from a man's hand in a pub. Even an outdoor one. It's definitely *not* the place for it." He watched her fingers dance above the plate until she chose a perfectly sized chip to eat.

"Where is the right place?" she asked.

His words lodged in his throat as she tucked the bite-sized chip between her lips and sucked the salt from her fingertips on the way out. He knew she didn't mean to taunt him, but no matter what she put in or pulled out of her mouth, he was mesmerized.

He fisted his hands beneath the table and leaned back on the bench, looking away. Toward the large Tí Joe Watty's sign painted on the building. Toward the horse-drawn cart going by on the paved road. Toward the several patrons sitting at the other picnic tables, chatting. Toward anything but her.

"Leif, you have about five seconds to say something halfway intelligible before I haul you over my shoulder to Doctor O'Donnell's."

He looked at her from the corner of his eye, amused that she'd quoted him verbatim. "All I know is the right place isn't here." He stood up and lifted his feet one by one over the picnic seat. "I'm getting another Guinness. You want another tequila sunrise?"

She popped a third chip in her mouth and shrugged. "Nah, I'm good."

"That you are."

****

Lorraine was so happy, she was nearly giddy. She

hadn't spoken out of her head or had any crazy visions since she'd awoken this morning. And more importantly, everything seemed to be going well between her and Leif. Maybe even a little too well.

Neither of them needed a relationship, especially a long-distance one. Because of his livelihood, Leif was probably a man who needed to pack up and travel at a moment's notice. Being tied down to a woman who lived across the sea would seriously put a strain on the independent lifestyle he was used to.

She then considered her recent breakup. The last thing she needed was to jump into another relationship with a man who could never commit. She'd wasted too many years of her life walking down that fruitless path already to do it again. It was time to blaze a new trail.

Plus, Patrick would kick her behind for leaping headlong into another unhealthy affair. She could just hear it... *You can't go falling in love with the first man who pays you attention, Raine. I know you're starving for it, but just 'cause he seems interested, doesn't mean he's interested in* you. *Most men will say almost anything to make you believe they care.*

As she ate her lunch, she thought about Leif and all the charming things he'd said to her since they first met: *"To let a poor, injured beauty like yourself wander the craggy fields of the Erin in a terrible storm...well, that wouldn't be very noble of me, now would it?"*

"You're welcome to stay as long as you like."

"It's his loss...and my gain."

Each one was better than the last. Did that mean they were all attempts to win her over and make her believe he cared? "I wonder..." she murmured.

"Wonder what?"

Leif's voice startled her as he circled the table with a

drink in hand. "Um…I was wondering…" Trying to make up something on the fly proved difficult as he flashed that sexy bright smile. He made her heart flutter, and everything else went haywire. She tried again. "I was wondering where we're going after lunch. I mean, what's next on the tour?"

"Do you have some place in mind?"

"You're the expert. What are some recommended places of interest on this isle?"

"Depends on what you're interested in. If you're a woman who just likes to ooh and aah over castle ruins, megaliths, and scenic cliffs…then we can go just about anywhere. But if you'd like to learn something as you go, then I've got a few locations I think you might enjoy."

Lorraine picked up a fried potato and dipped it in tartar sauce before eating it. "Care to guess which woman you think I am?"

Leif leaned forward and stole a chip from her plate. "I don't usually speculate anything. I'm a researcher, and I conclude findings based on facts, not presumptions."

"Chicken."

Leif laughed. "Maybe. Or perhaps it's my way of keeping you around longer. You forget, I enjoy research. I enjoy digging deep and finding things out on my own. It's what I do."

"And what if you don't like what you find?" Yeah, she was baiting him. But she wanted to know.

"I don't think that's going to happen."

"I thought you didn't speculate about things, Leif."

He slid his hand across the surface of the table and covered hers. "That's not me guessing," he stated, his voice as rich as dark chocolate. "That's a gut feeling."

Chapter Eleven

The hours in the day flew by, and before Lorraine knew it, it was nearly five o'clock. Leif had taken her to many historic sites on the island: the eighth-century St. Edna's Church, tucked away amid the dunes and sawgrass, and what was left of St. Benen's Church sitting high atop a ridge near the remains of a round tower and holy well. At each location, he'd rattle off intriguing facts about the site, the people who built it, and the influence it had on the island as a whole.

Everything he'd explained, whether it be truth or legend, held her utmost attention. He was obviously well-versed in the island's history, and he knew how to narrate without making it feel like a boring college lecture.

It didn't hurt that her tour guide was ruggedly handsome and built like a linebacker. At moments when they'd dismount to get a closer look at medieval ruins, she took pleasure in the slight pressure of his hand at the small of her back, steadying her as she walked over the rocky ground. She felt as if no one was there on the isle with her, save him. She barely noticed the shifts of backpackers coming off the pier throughout the day or the occasional straggling tourist walking into her camera sights.

To escape the crowds, he finally took her to a remote part of the isle where the road eventually disappeared and the terrain became too dangerous for the horses. On foot, Leif guided Lorraine toward the great Dún Dúchathair. Left lonely and vulnerable, the ancient fort rested on a jagged outcrop stretching out toward the sea. It looked as if the island's bedrock had fallen away around it, leaving it to fend off the severe gales and crashing Atlantic waves below all by itself.

Lorraine stood in awe as Leif stood beside her, adjusting a pack he had brought and slinging it over his shoulder. "Amazing, isn't it?"

"Where is everyone? There's not a soul here."

Leif stretched out his arm and ushered her forward over the uneven earth. "It's just you, me, and the herons."

"Is it like this all the time?"

"Pretty much," he said with a nod. "Most people come to Inishmore for the more famous Dún Aonghasa and only a few knowledgeable tourists are aware this fort even exists."

Lorraine glanced behind her. "So, what's with the cantle bag?"

"You'll see."

She knew the pack contained the enigmatic can of whipped cream, but her curiosity over the bag's other contents dwarfed in comparison to the spectacular view before her. Clicking her camera as she went, Lorraine captured the stark beauty of the aged stronghold behind a backdrop of vibrant blue sky and puffy white clouds. She even snapped a few pictures of Leif standing at the cliff's edge, his blond hair blowing in the breeze. With his hands on his hips, his jaw set, and his eyes on the distant horizon, he looked like a king—a Norse warrior chieftain who gazed out over his newly conquered land and stood proud, fulfilled.

Leif realized he was being watched and turned around.

"What are you doing?"

She felt the heat of his gaze as he came near. "Taking your picture. Is that all right?"

"I've got a better idea." He seized the camera from her hands, and after a few seconds of glancing over the buttons, he held the camera up and zoomed in on her face. "Picture perfect."

"Quit," she warned, blocking the lens.

Leif backed up and rotated the camera, off-centering the harsh stone fort and the crashing sea to her left. "Oh, this would make a great black-and-white."

Lorraine tried to grab for the camera, but he lifted it out of her reach. She stood with her hands planted on her hips, but a smile betrayed her efforts at looking stern. "Seriously, can I have my camera back?"

He smiled so big, it reached his eyes. "I'm helping you document your trip. I want you to be able to look back on these photos and remember you were actually here." No sooner had those words fallen from his mouth, his laugh lines disappeared and his eyes darkened as he stared at her. "I want you to remember you were here with me."

"I don't think I'll ever forget that."

"You might," he said matter-of-factly. "Unless..."

Lorraine saw his gaze drift downward over her lips, though he made no effort to move. She could almost bet that he wanted to. She swallowed. "Unless what?"

A tiny grin teased his lips, and he inched closer. There was nothing she wanted more than to feel Leif's kiss. After all she'd been through with Brad, she deserved it. She dug deep down for courage and stepped into him, placing her hands on his chest. The solid wall of muscle beneath her palms did crazy things with her mind, and the heat through his T-shirt singed her fingertips.

"Unless what, Leif?"

He curled his arm around the small of her back and pulled her against him, peering deep into her soul. "Most people forget things unless they've experienced something memorable at the time. You might forget you were here with me, unless I brand it in your memory somehow."

Her heart fluttered like butterfly wings, but she remained as calm as she could, holding fast to the hope that he'd take the leap and kiss her. "I think you're right. I think I will forget this whole vacation…this entire day…unless you…" She wanted to say *unless you kiss me, dammit* but instead, she closed her eyes and held her breath.

She froze as I drew near. I lingered just short of her mouth, tipped her chin upward, and took her lips in a tender, gradual kiss, a sweet compromise of patience and passion.

Leif pulled away, unsure of what he felt or what he saw behind closed eyes. He couldn't explain it. The moment he pressed his lips to Lorraine's, an image of her flashed before him. But she looked different. Her style of hair and clothing were not of this time period. They weren't even of this century.

"What's wrong?" she asked.

He stepped back, separating himself from her touch. If he read her right, she seemed to have seen something as strange as he did. "Did you…?" He stopped mid-sentence, unable to put what he saw into words.

"Did I what, Leif?"

He took another step backward and ran his hand over his jaw. "That was very weird."

Confusion and pain surfaced in Lorraine's eyes, and as soon as she turned away from him in tears, he instantly realized his mistake. "Raine," he said, reaching for her. "That came out wrong."

"You don't have to explain." She shrugged him off.

"Yes, I do. Please. That wasn't what I meant at all." He tried to think of how to explain what he felt. There was a familiarity in the way she smelled, the way she tasted, the way she melted against him. Every part of that kiss was as known to him as the sensation of his own hands rubbing against his skin. It was like kissing her for the thousandth time and for the first. How was that possible?

Leif circled her, trying to separate his emotions from hers. He hung her camera around his neck by its strap and grasped her shoulders, forcing her attention away from the sea. "Your kiss was amazing. I've never felt anything like it." He grappled for something logical, desperate for sensible words, then a nervous laugh escaped him. "I've no idea how to describe what I felt when I kissed you. All I know is that I saw you, a different version of you. An ageless version of you. And as I gazed upon your face, I felt like I was out of my body—watching me kiss you. Does that make sense?"

Lorraine gawked at him for longer than he cared to admit, and it seemed like nothing registered by way of his description. What he tried to explain could only be described as ridiculous. Phenomena such as that happened only in far-fetched paranormal movies. Not real life.

After many uncomfortable seconds passed, he cut the tension by handing back her camera and apologizing. "Forgive me."

Slow and easy, she took the camera. "Forgive you for what?"

He rolled his eyes. "For my crude language, for one. And for ruining this moment."

"You didn't ruin it."

"Of course I did. Although, you must admit, I certainly made our first kiss into something you'll never forget," he said sarcastically. "For the record, that was definitely not how I wanted you to remember it."

Chapter Twelve

As Leif went to stand at the cliff's edge, Lorraine's stomach climbed into her throat. She wanted to admit she felt the same thing he did when they'd kissed, and that perhaps they'd both experienced some sort of bizarre déjà vu. But she feared he'd only think her crazy.

Being an archeologist, she'd bet he heard his fair share of curses and spells for unearthing sacred graves, but she also bet he never thought twice about it. He was a grounded, sensible man. It wasn't his style to believe in such madness.

Determined to help salvage his sanity as well as the rest of their evening, she picked up his cantle bag and walked over to where he stood. "I don't know about you, but I'm willing to call it even. You and I have had some really strange things happen since we met, and we've spoken even stranger things to each other. Maybe it's best we forget all that and start over." She handed the pack to him. "Truce?"

His looked at her, then accepted the bag. "I'd like that."

"Good." She fed her head through the camera strap and crossed her arms. "So, are you gonna show me what's in the cantle bag once and for all, or do I have to guess?"

Leif glanced at his watch and then to the horizon. "I suppose we can get ready."

"Get ready for what?"

She suspected he was still troubled by the kiss and its

bizarre development thereafter as he'd lost his cheerful mood, but nonetheless, he tried to smile. "You'll see."

Leif set the pack on the ground and unzipped it. The first item he removed was a blanket. Then a lighter. And then a candle. He spread the blanket on the ground at the edge of the cliff and lit the candle. "Have a seat."

She did as he bid her, still unsure of his motive and what he was preparing for. To her delight, he sat beside her, crossed-legged, but kept the cantle bag concealed behind him.

"Here, hold this."

He handed her a Ziploc bag of what looked like brown sugar and continued with his task, offering no other hint as to what he was doing. One by one, he pulled out items and set them on the blanket before them: a small bottle of Jameson whiskey, a bottle of Bailey's Irish liqueur, a thermos, two collapsible cups with lids, and of course the inexplicable can of whipped cream.

As an expert of mixed drinks, she eyed the ingredients and made her conjecture. "Are we making Irish coffees?"

"We are in Ireland." He stopped in the middle of opening the Bailey's. "Wait. Don't tell me you're one of those health addicts who doesn't drink coffee?"

"Are you kidding? I love coffee. Let's do this," she said excitedly. "'Course, the way I drink it, Patrick calls it coffee-flavored creamer."

"Is that the ex?" he asked, taking the bag of brown sugar from her hand.

"Oh God, no," she said. "Patrick's a good friend of mine. I've known him all my life. In fact, he's the one who insisted I come here to get away from Brad."

"Brad's the ex, then."

Hating to admit it, she cringed before she clarified. "Ex-fiancé."

A glint of pity flickered across his face, but he moved on. The constant motion of his hands kept her mesmerized, and she was thankful for the distraction. Though it didn't take much skill to prepare a drink, Leif had a way of making it entertaining. With fanciful, fluid twists, he poured some Bailey's into a lid and the brown sugar into another. After that, he dipped one of the cups into the liqueur and then into the brown sugar and rotated the brim in the granules. "Here's one," he said, presenting her with the sugar-coated cup.

"Most bartenders don't do it this way. It's not authentic, and it's too much trouble."

"Well, I'm not a bartender, and this is just the way I prefer to make them."

As she held her cup, he did the same with his, then gave it to her to hold. "So, if Patrick's such a great friend, why didn't he come here with you...if you don't mind me asking?"

"He was going to, but I turned down his offer."

Leif's brow lifted as he divided the thermos of coffee between the two cups. "Why is that?"

"Because he doesn't need to be here with me while he has a girlfriend at home."

"I see." He added the shots of Jameson to the coffee and another question popped out of his mouth. "Hypothetically, if Patrick didn't have a girlfriend, would you have wanted him to come with you?"

She knew where this was going. She exhaled. "Leif, I don't have a boyfriend, and I don't wish Patrick to be one either. He's practically like a brother to me—an older protective brother."

He poured some Bailey's into his cup, then hovered the bottle over hers. "I'm assuming you want this."

Lorraine noticed how smoothly he bypassed her reference of Patrick. After such a strong question, she expected something more out of him than a statement about cream liqueur. "Yes, please."

He gave her a generous measure and set it aside. "Now, for the moment you've been waiting for." He picked up the can of whipped cream and gave it a good shake.

Mindful of the full cups of hot coffee in each of her hands, she leaned forward and cast him an expectant look. "Hit me."

"Bottoms up." He held the nozzle above her open mouth and dispensed a huge dollop of cream on her tongue. Watching it curl in her mouth must have incited his naughty, playful side, and he continued to hold it down until it filled her mouth. She tried to hold it all in, and they both laughed as it seeped from between her lips and down her chin.

"Hold on," he said before she could swipe it away with her tongue. "I got this."

She swallowed what was in her mouth and froze as he caught the cream with his finger. His touch heightened every nerve in her body, especially when he licked it off his fingertip. He hummed over the delicious taste, and she inwardly found herself doing the same. She wanted to kiss his ever-perfect lips again and taste the sweet flavor of cream on his tongue.

"So, what's the verdict?" she asked, handing him his cup of Irish coffee. "Am I worthy of knowing the date of your birth? You know, the one saved only for your closest friends?" His fingertips brushed against hers in the transfer, and his eyes remained glued to her.

"I think it's a tossup, really."

"Let me guess. Speculating is out of the question, and you have to do more research before you decide."

He raised his glass. "You learn quickly."

"Then, here's to thorough research," she said, raising hers. "May we never forget the importance of persistence and due diligence."

"Nice," he crooned, clinking his plastic cup against hers.

Together, they took their first sip, and something held their gazes fixed. Maybe it was the expectation of another kiss hovering in the atmosphere, or the pull of the obvious attraction between them. Either way, Lorraine enjoyed every moment she sat there, lost in his eyes.

As the hours ticked by, their conversations altered from family and hobbies to embarrassing moments and miffs. Before long, she was three drinks in when the sun started to make its descent into the watery horizon.

"It's nearly time," he announced, taking her empty cup and setting it aside. "Trust me, you don't want to miss this."

As she followed the direction of his nod, she realized he was talking about the sunset. The brilliant, fiery sphere dangled above a rippling blanket of golden sea, and the surrounding sky burst with colorful shades of amber and bronze behind pink clouds. She'd seen many captivating sunsets in her time, but none equaled this one. Consumed by its beauty, she didn't even know Leif had moved behind her. It wasn't until he blocked her line of sight with her own camera that he broke her trance.

"I'm thinking you'll want to capture this."

"Oh, right," she said, clumsily taking hold of the device. "Thanks." As she focused in on the dimming sun, reflecting on the ocean, she could feel Leif's presence at her back. He wasn't touching her in any way, but he was close enough that if she leaned slightly backward, she'd be nestled against his chest.

Oh, what she wouldn't give to feel his strong embrace again, and it took everything she had to keep from easing back. The notion of his hard, muscular body only inches away from hers monopolized her every thought.

"It's beautiful, Leif. I'm so glad you brought me here."

"Mm-hm..."

Lorraine's breath caught. Leif was no longer inches behind her, but close enough that she could see his face in her peripheral vision at her shoulder. She didn't dare look at him, for if she moved at all, they'd bump noses.

He cupped her jaw and directed her to face him. It was incredible what this man could do to her. With barely a caress, he aroused her to the point of thrumming, and she could hear her heartbeat in her ears. In his eyes, she recognized a storm brewing, a *should I do this or not?* kind of disturbance, then he nudged her nose with his.

"I like you here with me," he whispered. "Everything is better with you here."

I barely got a word out before he lifted another piece of fruit to my lips.

"I like you here with me," Dægan said, then sucked his finger. The same one she'd put in her mouth. "Everything is better with you here."

Lorraine drew in a ragged breath. She'd somehow flitted away into another flashback at the sound of Leif's words. Familiar words he—no…Dægan—had said to her. As her vision faded, she no longer gawked at the Viking warrior, but at Leif.

Thankfully, Leif was none the wiser of her short disappearing act.

"It's all right," he comforted, still cupping her cheek. "I want to. I want to try this again. Will you let me?"

It was either kiss Leif or freak out about another ill-timed blackout. The answer was obvious.

"You've not answered me, Raine."

"You've not answered me, princess," he teased, wrenching me closer to smell the oils upon my skin beneath my jaw.

"H-how can I answer you?" I shuddered as I felt the slight tickle of his beard.

"Just open your mouth and speak."

Before I could utter one word of resistance, he skimmed his lips over my chin and covered my mouth with a kiss. I couldn't move, for it was the first time I'd ever experienced one in all my nineteen years. The world around me ceased to exist as the heat and red-blooded strength of his arms molded me tightly to his chest.

I fell limp in his arms and welcomed the gentle caresses of his tongue parting my lips. He went deeper, tasting me, but was never rough or demanding. He only eased his tongue in as much as I'd allow. He played with me, pulled away, then delved back in, taking every sweetened gasp from me like a thief.

I couldn't help but respond to his every touch, and my virgin tongue dared to dance with his. He moaned softly in my mouth, a noise hardly to be heard, but it was enough to make me open my eyes and find his swirling in drunken lustfulness.

His unashamed forwardness would've sent me fleeing, but his embrace enveloped me with a passion I'd never felt before. A strange heat burned low in my stomach, and a rush of cool shivers trickled down my spine as his kiss fed both of those glorious feelings at once.

"Are you all right?" Leif asked as he pulled out of the kiss. "You look frightened, Raine."

Chapter Thirteen

Lorraine blinked repeatedly. The momentous scene dissipated before her eyes. "I'm...I'm fine," she lied.

Leif smiled like a spent man savoring the moment. "I wish I could say the same. My heart is hammering in my chest."

Lorraine closed her eyes tight, trying to grasp it all. Through another crazy vision, she felt as though she'd experienced her very first kiss with her imaginary Viking lover, only the Norse warrior wasn't Leif. Or was it?

"Did we kiss?"

Leif drew back.

Of course we kissed. Lorraine backpedaled. "I mean, was this kiss better?" She swallowed, hoping she'd adjusted her question enough so she didn't look like a complete idiot.

Leif laughed and pulled her into his arms. "Don't be silly, love. Both kisses were amazing. I know I may have pulled away the first time, but it was because an uncanny emotion came over me...as if I've kissed you many times before." She heard him scoff. "We both know that's impossible."

Clinging to the security of his warmth, she burrowed into the solid protective wall of his embrace and tried to pull together her discombobulated brain. As far as she could gather, she saw things from a previous life—her previous life. As a princess in love with a Viking warrior.

The thought sounded completely absurd.

"So, what's your take on why it feels like you've kissed me before?" she asked, hoping Leif would have a scientifically sound explanation for what had come over him. Maybe it would shed light on what came over her.

"There's only one explanation. We're connected. In here." He pressed his palm to her chest. "I felt its hold on me when I first saw you at Dún Aonghasa. You looked strangely familiar, almost smelled familiar. I swear I should've known you. After kissing you, I feel it stronger than ever—and I think you do too. Maybe I'm fundamentally deranged saying all this, but I've got a gut feeling about us, and I'm running with it. Hell, just the other day, I had a gut feeling and it proved to be—" He stopped with a sudden blank expression on his face.

Lorraine reached up for his face with both hands. "What? It's proved to be what, Leif?"

He peered into her eyes, hesitating. He had a firm grip on both her arms, and she could sense a slight vulnerability in his gaze as if he wanted to say more but shouldn't. As though pulled from a deep train of thought, Leif glanced down at his hands. "You're trembling. You must be cold," he said, changing the subject. "Come on, I'll take you home."

****

Leif couldn't believe how close he'd come to slipping. He'd almost told her about the impulsive intuition that led him to dig and find the chest; the chest that he swore he'd never tell a soul about, the chest that he made his brother swear on in secrecy. But there was something about Lorraine that made him want to tell her everything, to divulge every little secret he ever had. He trusted her that much.

In the long six-mile trek back to his cottage, he had all kinds of time to think it over. But in the last mile, he realized he was no closer to figuring out whether it was a good idea to share his discovery or just plain premature and reckless. He groaned aloud before he was aware he'd been heard.

"Everything all right?"

Leif cleared his throat and shifted uncomfortably in his saddle, which then gave him the perfect excuse. "Yeah, I think I might need a new saddle. This one isn't as comfortable as it used to be."

Lorraine hung her head. "Would it have anything to do with the fact that it got ruined last night?"

"Not at all," he reassured her. "This saddle used to be my grandfather's before he gave it to my father, and so on. So, it's bound to have lost its comfort by now."

"Saddles are supposed to get better with age."

"To an extent. But everything has a breaking point. Nothing lasts forever."

"Some things do."

There was a peculiar tone in her voice when she said that, and Leif couldn't let it go by unnoticed. "Like what?"

She regarded him curiously. "Like…love."

"Love, huh? Like the love you felt for Brad?" He was cruel to have asked her with such condescension, but he wanted to know.

"What I felt for Brad wasn't love."

She sounded convincing, but it hardly clarified anything. "So, let me get this straight. You were going to marry someone you didn't love?"

"I was going to marry someone I *thought* I loved. And I

thought he loved me."

Leif was more careful about his choice of words. "Did he tell you he loved you?"

"Many times," she replied. "I should've known it wasn't sincere. Everyone else knew. But I just couldn't see it."

"Perhaps you didn't want to see it."

Her eyes darkened. "I prefer to think I was blind."

Leif laughed. "We're weaving through all kinds of clichés tonight, aren't we? Love is forever, love is blind. Next, you'll be telling me that love and hate are two horns on the same goat."

"You don't believe in love?" she asked.

He paused and chose his words carefully. "I believe in small blessings. Good fortune that happens to come our way."

"You mean like fate?"

"No, I mean like luck. If you happen to find love at all."

"So, all that talk about being connected was bullshit?"

Leif sensed the bitterness in her tone. He trotted up close, stole her reins, and halted their horses. "I meant what I said about having a connection with you. It's there, I know it's there, but I can't give you a rational explanation for it. Like I said at the fort, I'm running on gut instinct here. Nothing more. So, if you wish to call my gut instinct fate or destiny or even doom for that matter, so be it. But know this. I don't need a technical term to say I've met the woman I've always wanted."

****

They'd finally made it back to Leif's barn before the rain came down, sparing the leather and saddle pads from a watery demise. Lorraine had ridden enough times with Patrick to know that waterlogged blankets and horse sweat emitted an unpleasant smell. As they untacked each of the horses, the rhythm of rain outside did little to douse her emotions. Although Leif was in the next stall, she could feel a sense of heavy unrest between them because of the surprising nature of Leif's last comment. The subject had been left to hang in the balance, and her world was caught in a virtual tailspin. *"I don't need a technical term to say I've met the woman I've always wanted."*

How could he decide something so definite after only knowing her for a little over twenty-four hours? She didn't have to pose that question to know he'd probably answer with the same, ever-familiar "gut feeling" excuse. While that might be enough for Leif, it wasn't enough for her. If she truly was the woman he'd always wanted, she expected, and deserved, more than just a hunch.

On the other hand, she adored Leif's spontaneity, his blunt openness, and his bold charm. He kept her on pins and needles, and he was always unpredictable. All her life, she'd been waiting for someone like him, but was she ready for another commitment? It had been less than a week since she'd dumped her fiancé, and Leif was worth so much more to her than a rebound guy.

She carried the heavy saddle and pad into the tack room and placed them on the rack, purposefully avoiding Leif's gaze. Despite her desire to be near him, she'd convinced herself to say thanks for the wonderful day and then good night. She needed time to think and to make certain her head was screwed on tight. As difficult as separating from him sounded, she knew it was the right thing to do.

After straightening the stirrups and tidying up the girth and buck straps, she turned to fetch the bridle and reins she left hanging over the stall gate. Just as she exited the tack room, Leif was entering, and they collided.

He smiled. "In a hurry to go somewhere?"

Backing up, she collected her thoughts. "Yeah, I should go. To my B&B, I mean." A nervous laugh staggered out. "I haven't even slept in the bed I've paid for."

He stepped forward, blocking her only means of escape. "Whether you sleep there or not, it's the same price."

"I know, but I need a shower and—"

"I've got a shower." He took another step toward her until he'd backed her against the barn wall, and braced his arm above her head. "A shower large enough for two."

Tipping her head back, she looked him in the eye. She couldn't argue with him, as his shower *was* big enough for two. "But I don't have any clean clothes."

"Seriously? That's your excuse?"

She felt as if the oxygen around her was depleting. "Yes, I am. I need clean clothes—my own clothes," she amended. "And a good night's sleep."

He cupped her jaw and ran his thumb over her bottom lip. "Stay with me, Raine," he whispered. "Stay." He bent and kissed her. The smell of him tempted her to give in, and the taste of his lips suppressed any shred of will power she had left. But the feel of his strong, masculine hand snaking around her waist and cupping her bottom until she was pressed firmly against him sealed the deal. All hope of resisting Leif Dæganssen vanished.

Chapter Fourteen

A hardened palm rolled me to my back and another covered my mouth. It was Dægan, his dagger in hand. The blade reflected an evil shine from the fire, and his eyes expressed a gravity as heavily as the day they saw the four ships with red and white sails. He brought a finger to his lips, demanding my absolute silence, and then pointed outside.

"We have company," he whispered. "Stay here."

I sat up to object, but he pushed me back down and brought his face so close to mine that his lips touched my cheek as he spoke. "I said lie still. They don't know I'm with you. Let them think that."

"What will you do?"

Dægan grabbed my trembling hand and placed the dagger within it, but didn't answer me. He unsheathed his sword in the very slowest of ways and quietly backed up with the same careful stealth, putting his finger to my lips one last time before the shadows of the cavern swallowed him whole.

Panic gripped me. I couldn't breathe. Disturbing images of foreigners numbering in the hundreds, fully clad in armor and helmets, flashed before me. Pictures of heathen men wielding bloody swords and mighty battle-axes drained the blood from my body like a sieve.

The rustling came again, but closer now as if they were just outside the opening. My heart slammed to a stop. I searched the darkness, trying to see through the teeming rain. It was useless. How could Dægan leave me like this?

Two men suddenly emerged, their swords drawn, their steps cautious. They dripped from head to toe, and their warm breath emitted like dragon's fire into the cool air.

I *concealed the dagger I'd been given and waited as Dægan had told me. It was evident now that they believed me to be alone, for they lowered their weapons and stalked toward the fire.*

"Well, well," one said resignedly. "You're a hard little wench to track down."

I sat deathly still, looking from one to the other.

"She's in here!" the man called over his shoulder. His voice echoed against the damp rock walls, and at that instant, Dægan came out of the shadows. He slashed fatally across the one man's back and turned about to take on the other. The second man barely got his sword raised before Dægan thrust his blade so deep into the man's stomach that it exited his back. Dægan held his forearms extended until the man slid from the blade and fell to the ground. Dægan glanced at me, then slipped back into the shadows.

Dægan's horse shifted about inside the cavern, and I jumped up to calm the nervous animal. As I stroked its muzzle and neck, three more men ran into the cavern.

They stopped in their tracks and found their comrades dead at their feet with only me in the firelight, my little weapon in hand. Their eyes widened in astonishment and their expressions turned angry and callous.

"You want to play rough, aye?"

I turned to face them head-on and kept one hand on the horse's back. I prepared myself for yet another brutal attack, only this time Dægan came from the opposite side of the cavern.

He slew the first unsuspecting victim with ease and ducked to avoid the coming of a high sword at his head. As he stood up, he spun and cut the second man deeply across the thighs, making ready to take on the third. He let the Northman initiate the duel. Their irons clanged in the night, until Dægan forced the man's sword tip into the ground and stepped on it. He came up swiftly to cut the unguarded throat of the Northman. As that man dropped like a sack of wheat,

Dægan revisited one of the wounded, double fisted the hilt above his head, and staked his sword deep into his foe's chest.

The grotesque sight of a broad blade sinking deep into tender flesh pulled Lorraine out of her nightmare, and she bolted upright in bed, taking the covers with her. Still trying to get the cries of wounded men out of her head, she searched her surroundings and realized she wasn't in the tenth century, but in bed with Leif.

"It's okay," he soothed as she panted. "It's just a dream, Raine, it's just a dream." She'd jolted him awake with her scream, and he held her close in a warm, sheltering embrace. She clung to him, relishing the heat of his bare chest and the solid strength of his arms. She closed her eyes and tried to pull it all together, concentrating on the glorious sensation of naked skin on skin and the love they'd made last night. Falling asleep in his arms was the image she wanted to memorize, not the violent ones from her nightmare.

As she opened her eyes, she saw a hideous scar on Leif's left thigh and scrambled out of the bed in a hurry.

"Raine, what's wrong?" he asked, scooting across the mattress after her.

She tripped over her own feet to get away and crashed to the floor, crab-walking into the corner. Sheer terror enslaved her as her surroundings spun within a blurry haze. The last she saw was Leif padding toward her.

I rushed to Dægan's side, looking him up and down. "You're hurt!"

He glanced at himself as if surprised that his upper thigh had been sliced open. "Naught but a flesh wound."

I didn't appreciate his lighthearted humor, and a few tears escaped me.

"Are you all right?" he asked.

"Nay, I'm not all right," I sobbed. "You could have been killed."

Dægan wrapped his free arm around me and attempted to make light of the situation. "Not likely with you on my side."

I was sure he half expected me to evade his reach, but I didn't. I stayed where he'd drawn me and felt good in his embrace. Natural. As if the small of my back was made just for the crook of his arm.

He must have felt my body tremble, for he then sheathed his sword. "Come by the fire and warm yourself. Come, now."

He guided me far beyond the fallen men and made sure to hide the gruesomeness, tucking me into the concave space beneath his shoulder.

I sat where he deemed so and stared about the dancing flames, still in shock at the carnage. "Did you know those men?"

Dægan circled the fire and fetched his bear cloak from the ground, draping it around my shoulders. "Aside from assuming they were the men we encountered on the banks of the River Shannon, I cannot say I know them at all."

"Did you see how they looked at you? 'Twas as if they knew you or—had seen you before."

"I saw it in their eyes as well. But I tell you in truth, I knew them not."

He sat beside me and pulled the bearskin cloak tighter around my shoulders to keep out the cold of the night and the chill of death. It was then that my concern for his wound escalated. Blood had already seeped into the hem of his kirtle, a red so dark, it looked black in the shadows of the cavern. It trailed a wide path down toward his knee and around his outer thigh.

"You're bleeding," I said. "A great deal…"

Before Dægan could argue differently, I took the hem of my gown and dabbed at the blood oozing from his leg. Gingerly at first, as I was nervous to even touch him, but more fixedly as he continued to bleed. Soon, I employed both hands.

"You don't wear breeches like the other men," I said absently.

"In Hladir," he explained, "'tis a necessity, for the winds are cold enough to turn a man's skin black. But here, the weather is tolerable. I've grown accustomed to the way the men of the Erin dress. I prefer it, actually."

By the time he finished his explanation, I'd become so absorbed in cleaning his wound that I didn't even realize how high I'd wiped up his leg, just short of grazing him. He quickly gathered my hands in his.

I glanced up, and a well of near-falling tears pooled in my eyes. "Did I hurt you?"

"Of course not."

"But you stopped me."

"Only because I've more than recovered. Thank you."

Lorraine fought to open her eyes, to put an end to the voices and scenes in her head. She could hear Leif's voice talking to her, his arms holding her against him, stroking her hair. But something gripped her and pulled her back, forcing her out of Leif's guest room and into a tattered animal-skin tent lit by torches. She jerked and heaved to get away but found ropes bound tightly around her wrists and a soiled gag tied around her face.

A man briskly entered the tent. He stood with legs spread, his shining sword marked with the color of violent death, and his flaxen hair curling from under his helmet. He removed it with one jerking motion and dropped it at his feet.

My stomach coiled and turned over. My breath stopped in my chest. My eyes fixed on Domaldr's awful face.

And he smiled.

The bastard smiled as if he'd just won me after a fierce tournament. As if he'd seen through Breandán's ruse and came to me in profound mockery, letting me see what was left of Breandán dripping from his blade and boasting the kill like a trophy.

He sheathed his bloody sword and yanked a dagger from his belt. Before he could take one step forward, I had already begun to crawl away.

He came down on top of me and rolled me over, holding me tightly in his arms. I screamed and writhed against his body, jerking sharply in hopes my knees would catch his groin.

He called my name and ordered me to be quiet, but I continued to thrash. His hard, cold armor and mail pushed sharply through my gown and against my legs as he sat upon me.

"Mara, 'tis me," he whispered forcibly. "Dægan."

Oh God, *I thought.* He's callous enough to use that trick again. How dare he. How dare he think me that stupid!

I cursed him behind the gag, a long slur of words quite unbefitting a woman, and if I could have spit at him, I would've done that too. Instead, I made doubly certain his effort to procure me was nothing short of difficult.

He grabbed my wrists now, yanking them up to the level of his eyes. I braced myself for his swift punishment and even welcomed the possibility of death before he could have his way with me.

"Hold still!" he commanded as he held the blade between my wrists. He paused only for a moment, then put the knife directly on the rope and pulled. My hands dropped free, and with animal instinct, I smacked for all I was worth.

"Mara, please listen to me. 'Tis I, Dægan. I swear it. Look at me."

I clenched my hand into an embittered fist and struck him

solidly, his head snapping to the right. He groaned and gripped both my hands, forcing them above my head as he pinned me to the ground.

"Look at me," he said again, but I squeezed my eyes shut on purpose. "Damnation, woman!" He plummeted to my ear and spoke in a gentled tone. "Shh…listen to my voice, love. Listen to it. I beg you."

I stilled for a brief moment, nauseated by the heated whisper upon my skin and cringing at the thought of Domaldr's putrid breath upon me. He made no effort to maul my neck as I thought he would. I narrowly opened my eyes, and through my desperate heavy panting, I smelled a hint of expensive oils, the familiar scent of his hair, and the faint masculine aroma of his leather armor.

I stared as he sat up. I wanted to believe with everything that was in me that this man was Dægan. That, through the impossible, my tried-and-true husband had found a way to travel across the sea and rescue me.

I studied his chest and broad shoulders, eyeing the thick shell of metal plates, leather, and ringlets around his torso and arms, but his armor looked nothing like Dægan's. I feared it was a trick. Almost felt in my heart that it was, and sucked in a breath for screaming, but he placed a gentle finger to my gagged mouth.

"Look at me," he whispered. "Listen closely to what I say to you, for there's not much time. You first gave yourself to me in Hlymrekr. And the next morning, I thought you regretted it, but you didn't. I can describe every part of you if you want me to. I can tell you how sweet your tongue is after you've sucked the sugar from my finger. I can count on one hand the times I made love to you and wish on my very life 'twere more. I can speak of the solitary freckle just beneath your right breast and the birthmark on your inner thigh, for only a husband could know such intimate things. I'm your husband. I want naught more than your love and trust right now and by the great God in Heaven, I wish I could steal it. But I won't. I'll wait forever and a day for you. Listen to my words, Mara, for I speak as a lost sheep.

Find me. Find me in your heart…I just might be there."

I felt the certainty in his words and the sweet ring of familiarity. No one could know those things save for Dægan himself. Relief and unfettered happiness washed over me like an ocean wave, though my words were trapped amid the shock of his very presence. As final proof of his true identity, I quickly lifted his kirtle and there, like a brand, was the wound across his left thigh he'd received a week ago in the cavern.

Lorraine's eyes fluttered open. Lazily at first, then as wide as she could muster after she realized a strange man was waving a tiny bright light back and forth in front of her. "Ms. O'Connor, can you hear me?"

She shoved the light away. "Of course, I can. Who are you?"

"I'm Dr. O'Donnell. Leif called me. He was worried about you."

Lorraine glanced at Leif sitting on the bed next to her and regarded the anxious lines furrowing his face. Upon seeing him shirtless in jeans, she recalled the last thing she remembered doing with him and jerked her gaze down over her body, fearing she too was without clothes. His oversized T-shirt adorned her naked body, and she was never so thankful. She sank back into the bed, feeling Leif squeezing her hand.

"It's okay now, Raine. You're safe."

"Ms. O'Connor," the doctor said as he sat down on the side of the bed. "Can you tell me what you remember?"

Lorraine looked back at Leif and swallowed. She remembered everything. The scar she found on his leg and the vision of how he came to be wounded. Only it wasn't Leif, but Dægan who acquired it.

She remembered the fight to the death. The blood. The sound of the dying men's screams. And she remembered caring for Dægan's wound thereafter, feeling guilty that he hurt himself while saving her. She then recalled the feeling of dread and hopelessness when she thought Dægan's twin was about to kill her, only to be relieved at seeing his wicked scar, proving he was her— Did she dare think it? *...for only a husband could know such intimate things. I'm your husband.*

Oh, she remembered it all.

She remembered her life as a Connacht princess, and living on the run for the next few weeks with her Viking protector. She remembered the journey to his home—here on Inishmore—and the burial of his younger brother Eirik. She remembered marrying Dægan before Irish and Norse witnesses at Dún Aonghasa and consummating their union in his longhouse near the beach. Of all the things she wished she could forget, she remembered his tragic death in her very arms.

Every aspect of her previous life, good and bad, had come back to her as if it happened yesterday. Her past was no longer an obscure parapsychological phantasm, but an increasingly lucid, mind-blowing memory. She was Mara, the daughter of Cathal Mac Conor, reincarnated.

"Ms. O'Connor?" the doctor said. "Think back. What do you remember?"

She looked between Dr. O'Donnell and Leif. Knowing they were likely gauging her for symptoms of insanity, she dared not say anything incriminating. "I don't know. It's all so..." She pretended to try to search for words.

"Don't try to force it," the doctor soothed. "It's likely not to come back to you." He turned to Leif now. "When a person suffers a concussion, their short-term memory is often affected. When did you say she fell?"

"Two days ago."

"Hmm."

"Actually," Leif corrected, counting in his head. "It was less than two days. More like thirty-two hours."

"So, that means we're still within the transitory forty-eight-hour period where anything is possible."

"What do you mean anything is possible?"

"I mean that dizziness, nausea, memory loss, confusion, and hallucinations are not out of the ordinary. Add a concussion on top of desynchronosis, and you're bound to acquire some sort of anxiety, irritability, insomnia, and even coordination problems." He patted Leif's knee and stood from the bed. "I don't think you have anything to worry about. Her pupils are reactive, her hematoma on her forehead is unchanged, and her color is good. I think she just needs some rest." The doctor shot Leif a look as though he knew about their late-night lovemaking. "I mean it, son. Let the woman rest."

Leif scratched his head self-consciously. "Right. Just send me the bill."

The doctor didn't wait to be let out and closed the door behind him.

Leif hung his head and sighed. "Thank God you're all right."

Lorraine sat up, rejuvenated. She cupped his cheek, amazed that her Dægan sat before her. Alive and well. She gazed into Leif's tired eyes. She'd seen that look before. Centuries ago, after he'd gallantly crossed over mountains and seas to save her from his malicious twin brother. He'd looked exhausted and drained from the mental stress he put on himself then as he did now.

Little did Leif know, she'd been given a gift. The gift of remembering her life as a tenth-century Irish princess in love with a Viking warrior, and being reunited with that very man in present time. Happier than she'd ever been, she stroked Leif's cheek. "You don't have to worry anymore. I'm fine."

Leif laughed. "Where have I heard that before?"

"I know it's hard to believe," she tried to explain, "but whatever happened tonight won't happen again. I'm sure of it."

His face turned somber. "What *did* happen tonight? From what I saw, you found my birthmark and freaked out. Is it that hideous?"

"Birthmark? That's what it is?"

"Ever since I came out of my mother's womb," he said matter-of-factly. "She wanted to have a plastic surgeon fix it, but my father refused. He said God put it there for a reason, and we shouldn't mess with what His hands have sculpted. So it stayed."

She glanced down at his thigh, recalling the mark hidden behind his jeans. "May I see it again?"

Leif furrowed his brow at her. "I don't think that's such a good idea."

"Please," she begged.

"With all due respect, Raine, I'm not in the mood to be a circus act."

Lorraine grabbed his wrist, keeping him from leaving. "I think it's a beautiful birthmark."

"So beautiful you crawled away in fright?"

Lorraine had no idea how to explain herself without making things worse. She had to speak carefully else she feared she'd lose him. "Actually, your birthmark helped me to feel relieved. Years ago, I was taken by a man—"

"Kidnapped?"

"You could say that," she said, biting her lip. "The man who saved me had a mark across his leg, just like you. I've never forgotten what it looked like."

"And seeing mine triggered those bad memories," he finished for her.

"Well, they weren't all bad. The brave man did save me."

Leif lifted her hand and kissed the inside of her wrist. "Another lovely cliché to add to our collection. The only one we're missing is 'and they lived happily ever after.'"

They gazed into each other's eyes, and an unspoken bond joined the two as if they'd found the other half of their soul and couldn't live another day without it.

"Will you hold me, Leif? I don't want to sleep alone."

He smiled. "I refuse to lie without you, love."

Chapter Fifteen

Kristoff opened the front door and leaned inside. "Leif? You home?" When his brother didn't answer, he stepped into the cottage and called again, this time loud enough to wake the dead, just for good measure.

"Well, what do we have here?" he said, taking notice of the trail of clothes left on the floor leading down the hall. Picking up what seemed to be a feminine shirt, he followed the path until he found a lacy article of clothing. Ditching the boring shirt for the more interesting item, he held it up, examining every aspect of the intimate apparel. He announced his approval. "Now, that's what I'm talking about, Leif."

Leif's guest room door flew open, and he stumbled into the hallway, half-asleep. His eyes were bloodshot and furious as he braced himself on the wall. Seeing Raine's bra twirling about on his brother's finger, he dashed forward and snatched it away. "Do you mind?"

Kristoff ignored him, his eyes lighting up as he peeked around Leif's shoulder. "She still in there? Naked?"

Irritated, Leif shut the door and dragged Kristoff into the kitchen, hitting him upside the head. "What the hell is wrong with you? Can't you at least act your age?" Leif stuffed Lorraine's bra into his back jeans pocket and started making coffee. He filled the glass pitcher with water and swore he'd just closed his eyes when his brother had rudely awakened him. "What are you doing here anyway?"

"We planned on working on the boat today, remember?"

Pinching the bridge of his nose, Leif recalled their conversation a few days ago. Hand-hewing planks of wood for Kristoff's hobby project was not something he cared to tackle this morning. "Does it have to be today?"

"Yes, it has to be today," Kristoff said, planting his bottom in the closest kitchen chair. "I'm booked solid all week, and this is the only day I'm free."

Leif looked over his shoulder. "Does that mean you won't be attending my birthday celebration at Joe Watty's?"

Kristoff laughed about the bogus birthday celebration. "That was quick thinking, wasn't it?"

Leif spooned in an additional scoop of grounds. He knew he was going to need it. "I would have rather you stayed out of it."

"Oh, come on. You know we would've been there anyway to celebrate your birthday, so it wasn't a total lie. It's just a little sooner than we thought."

Leif leaned against his counter and crossed his ankles. "So, how're the party plans coming? Have our imaginary guests RSVP'd yet?"

"Actually, they have. I put a call into Willie and Karen, and they said they'd try to make it. Mícheál and Catharina are in town. They said they'd swing by. Oh, and remember John and Kevy from Fretwear? They agreed to lug the ol' flat box down from Belfast and kick out a few Tommy Emmanuel tunes.

Leif shook his head. "How do you do it?"

"Do what?"

"You fall in a pile of shit and come out smelling like a rose, that's what."

"What can I say? No one can say 'no' to this face."

"I can." Leif pushed himself off the counter and grabbed two mugs from his cabinet. "And I'm telling you 'no' right now. I'm not working on that bloody boat today."

"Why not?"

"'Cause I'm tired."

Kristoff threw him an incorrigible grin. "Lorraine kept you up all night, huh?"

Leif sighed and glanced at the slow stream of liquid energy dripping from his coffeemaker. Kristoff was not going to let up. "We had a really nice ride yesterday, and before we knew it, it was late. Neither of us was ready to say good night."

"I'll bet."

"There's nothing wrong with two people enjoying each other's company, Kristoff."

"Ah, but in how many positions did you enjoy her?"

Leif ignored his brother.

"Please tell me you ventured a little and at least tried two."

Leif had no idea why he even attempted to have a decent conversation with Kristoff. Immaturity was his brother's downfall and always would be. It was no wonder he never had a steady girlfriend.

"Just give me a little sliver of detail. We're brothers."

"Exactly," Leif agreed. "What if one day she's your sister-in-law? Morally, her brother-in-law shouldn't want to know those kinds of details."

"Whoa, whoa, did you just mention..." His face scrunched up as if he had an awful taste in his mouth. "Marriage?"

"No."

"Yes, you did," Kristoff argued.

Leif paused, retracing his words. "I was speaking hypothetically."

"You were speaking as though you had your whole life planned out with a woman you met only two days ago."

Leif's first inclination was to dispute the preposterous allegations. He wasn't planning his life with Lorraine, nor was he contemplating marriage. Committed relationships and historical archeology required a strict obligation of time and dedication, and if one side demanded more of either disciplines, the other would inevitably suffer. Sustaining a healthy relationship in his career field seemed nigh on impossible. But as he methodically reached for the coffeepot, something as domestic as pouring two cups and living out his natural life with Lorraine felt right. With her, nothing seemed out of place or complicated.

"Bloody hell, Leif. You're actually giving this thought?"

Leif looked up from his coffee cup and found Kristoff standing beside him, drinking from the mug he'd poured for Lorraine. "That wasn't for you."

Kristoff held the cup out of Leif's reach. "Are you listening to anything I've said? You cannot marry this woman. You don't know her."

"And clearly you know what's best for me."

Kristoff took a huge gulp of coffee and swallowed quickly. "Damn right I do. I'm your brother. I know you better than anyone." He peered into his cup, frowning. "And I know American coffee's more like water, but you made this coffee so strong, it can walk."

Leif rolled his eyes and retrieved another mug from the cabinet. "You may be my brother, but you don't know me as well as you think. Heck, you don't even know where our ancestors originally came from, but she does."

"Trondheim."

"Yes, but more specifically Lade," he said, pouring another cup. "Or Hladir in Old Norse."

"What the hell does that have to do with the price of tea in China?"

"All I'm saying is you haven't the faintest idea what makes me tick."

"Just because you're suddenly intimate with this woman doesn't mean she knows what makes you tick either."

Leif opened his mouth to speak, then closed it, heat prickling up the back of his neck. "I'm done with this conversation." He turned and prepared Raine's coffee the way she liked it, lots of cream and sugar.

"Hey, look," Kristoff said. "I didn't mean to insult her. I like her. She seems like a great girl. I just don't want you to rush into anything." He took another generous swig as though he'd forgotten its strength, and grimaced. "I can't drink this shit."

Leif stole the mug from Kristoff's hands and dumped it out in the sink. "I put in a whole extra scoop today, and if you're going to continue to barge into my house, I'll keep making it that way from now on."

"You'd miss me after a while." Kristoff opened the fridge and pulled out a carton of eggs, a block of cheese, and milk, setting all the ingredients on the counter.

"What are you doing?"

"Making us some breakfast. After having your coffee, I'm sure as hell not eating your eggs."

Leif dragged his hands down his face. "Did it ever occur to you I have company?"

"Don't worry, I'll make her some too. I'm not that

rude."

Irritated, Leif grabbed the two coffee mugs and turned on his heel to check on Lorraine, almost barreling into her. He swiftly backed up to compensate for the shift in the sloshing coffee, then noticed her shapely bare legs sticking out from under his T-shirt. "Good morning."

She crossed her knees and pulled the shirt lower upon finding Kristoff in the kitchen. "I'm sorry, I didn't know—"

"It's okay, he's leaving."

But Kristoff made sure to blow holes into Leif's statement by cracking the first egg into a skillet. "I'm making breakfast, actually. Want some?"

Leif handed her a cup of coffee with a look of apology. "He does make good eggs."

Lorraine took the first sip of her coffee, still jerking the shirt down her thighs, and smiled. "I appreciate the offer, but I think I'm gonna head on out."

"You don't have to leave," Leif insisted. "I can kick him out. I'm not above using force."

"Oh no, I—"

"Please, Raine," Leif begged, closing his eyes. "Please, let me use force on my brother. I'll feel so much better." Her giggle sent him through the clouds, and the adorable way she wrapped both hands around her cup while sipping melted him into the hopeless romantic he told her he was.

"I really should go," she said again, setting her cup on the table and gesturing with a tilt of her head and a flick of her eyes in the direction of the hall.

Leif followed her out of the kitchen, and reached for her hand once they were beyond Kristoff's sight. He threaded his fingers with hers, yanked her into his embrace, then slowly backed her against the wall. "I can make him leave. Just say the word, and he's gone."

She took a slow deep breath as if to contemplate his suggestion. "I have things I need to do."

"Like what?" he asked, nuzzling her neck.

"Like charge my phone, in case I need it later today."

"Charge it here." He knew he was being overly persistent, but the knowledge that his shirt was the only thing standing between him and her naked body taunted him. The smell of her smooth, feminine skin didn't help matters either.

"I would, but my charger is in my suitcase along with the converter."

"I'll send Kristoff up the road for it and kill two birds with one stone."

She giggled softly in his ear. "You want Kristoff snooping around in my suitcase where all the rest of my bras and panties are?"

He groaned. "Then I'll fetch it."

She kissed his neck, her lips lighting his whole body afire. "I appreciate it, but I really need to call home. My phone is dead, and by now Patrick's probably conjured up all kinds of worst-case scenarios as to why he can't reach me. Plus, I want to run into Kilronan and buy one of those Aran sweaters. I've always wanted one."

Leif exhaled and released her, stepping back. He knew when he'd beaten a dead horse long enough. He took a sip of his coffee and looked her over one last time. "Need a lift into town?"

"Nah, I'll do what everyone else does. Rent a bike or something."

"Are you sure you feel well enough?" he asked, worried. "I don't like sending you off by yourself after last night."

"I promise. I feel wonderful."

He didn't push the issue, trying to take her at her word. "Can I see you tonight?"

"I'd like that."

"I can pick you up for dinner," he suggested.

Lorraine placed her hands on his bare chest, and her fingers plotted imaginary designs around his nipples as she laid out her plans. "How about I cook dinner for you here? And this time, I'll make sure to bring a change of clothes."

His heart leapt. "I like the sound of that."

"I'll swing by around seven?"

Leif thought of his brother's high hopes of working on the boat today. It looked as if he'd have time after all. "Seven's good."

She stood on her tiptoes and kissed him, the taste of rich coffee, sweet sugar, and ripe feminine lust abundant on her lips. It took everything he had to let her leave. He swallowed the urge to kiss her again, especially when she skimmed her hand around his waist and into his back pocket.

Smiling up at him, she pulled her bra free and held it up. "I think I'll need this."

"That, and your shirt, and your jeans," he said, pointing to the trail of garments that led from his living room to the spare bedroom. "And your socks, your raincoat…"

"Okay, okay, I got it." She giggled again.

He didn't mean to be lazy, but watching her pick up her strewn-about clothes from all parts of the house held his full attention. His shirt, to his delight, shortened in length every time she bent over, leaving nothing to the imagination. As she walked past him toward the bathroom, she tucked her sheer white thong in his front pocket.

"A souvenir for you." She winked.

Leif clenched his jaw. Seven o'clock couldn't come soon enough.

Chapter Sixteen

Showered and dressed, Lorraine tied her shoelaces and slipped her arms through her Lands' End jacket, ready to take on the world. In coming to Ireland, she'd left her troubles behind to find strength and independence. What she ended up discovering was she that wasn't meant to stay single after all. Whether it was God's intervention or a small blessing, as Leif would call it, she'd found the man she'd fallen in love with from another lifetime.

Not many people could claim such a thing. She knew a few who alleged to have lived previous lives, but they had little to no recognition of their past or those they came in contact with. Up until now, she'd thought them a little eccentric and, on some occasions, psychiatrically disturbed. She almost wished she'd paid more attention to their inconceivable stories. Maybe she'd have a better understanding of how it all worked and how, if possible, to jog another's past-life memory.

Though Leif didn't seem to recognize her from his past, he professed to have felt a connection with her, and that thread of optimism had her beaming with hope. If she could only stir his subconscious enough to let the deeply suppressed memories of his past resurface, as his birthmark had done for her, then perhaps there was a chance he'd recall the medieval life they'd shared.

Perhaps their first kiss might have sparked a faint memory from that period. She recalled his words: *"I've no idea how to describe what I felt when I kissed you. All I know is that I saw you, a different version of you. An ageless version of you. And as I gazed upon your face, I felt like I was out of my body—watching me kiss you."*

Then she recalled Dægan. He was such a beautiful man, with hair like the sun and eyes like the ocean. She remembered how strong, stubborn, and confident he was, and how he said he'd marry her with or without her father's consent. Leif was not quite the domineering fellow he once was as Dægan.

She blamed the affluent civilized society for taming the wild warrior within him. Men no longer claimed other men's daughters as their own, or married them to sustain peace, acquire power, and accrue wealth. They no longer drew swords to protect their families, defend their honor, or fight for freedom. Life was much easier now, and safer. The need for brave men, armed to the teeth, to save the damsel in distress had been all but whittled away to nothing.

Modern life had diluted the epitome of undaunted courage and chivalry. But no matter what sort of man contemporary society had nurtured Leif to be, she'd love him just the same.

As she pondered how to rekindle Leif's memory, she glanced at her phone that had been charging on the table since she entered her quaint accommodations at the Man of Aran Cottage. She saw three bars, good enough for making a quick call to Patrick before she headed into town, and the display that she'd missed three calls from him. She cringed, knowing an ass-chewing was inevitable, but pressed two anyway.

Pacing the room, she counted the rings before he picked up. One. Two. And a half. "Are you all right? How's your head? Where are you? Why haven't you picked up? I've called you about a hundred times—"

"Three, actually...and hello to you too, Patrick."

Lorraine heard him sigh. "Sorry. I was just worried. You said you'd call, and you didn't. Then, when I tried calling you, it went straight to voice mail. Just tell me you're all right and you're safe."

Lorraine sat on the edge of her bed, soothed by his familiar aura of concern. "I'm safe and sound. I've been safe ever since I last talked to you. I just forgot to charge my phone, and it was out of reach."

"What do you mean out of reach? Your luggage is with you, right? Don't tell me the airline lost it."

"My luggage is in my possession," she said reassuringly, but she wondered how she'd explain the rest. "Don't get mad, but in the past couple of days, I haven't been near my luggage."

A few seconds of silence spanned across the wire. "Where have you been?"

"I've been following your rules."

"What?"

"You gave me strict rules to follow while I was in Ireland, remember?" She ticked off one by one on her fingers. "No calling Brad. No turning in before the sun sets. No wallowing in self-pity. And, my personal favorite, do something crazy at least twice a week while I'm here." She laughed inwardly as she recalled her days spent with Leif. "Well, lookie there. I managed to do every single one of them."

Silence again followed.

"Patrick?"

"Who are you, and what have you done with my

Raine?"

Lorraine giggled and fell backward on the bed. Patrick was right. She was a completely new person, and she loved it. She felt liberated, confident, and daring, with a hint of sexy. Brad had never made her feel those things. If anything, he subdued her vitality for life, making her feel like a shrinking violet who'd not be worth a second glance.

Because of Leif, she remembered the girl who knew what it felt like to love and be loved in return. The stubborn female who wouldn't back down, and the determined woman who'd go after what she wanted. The person who dared to be adventurous, tenacious, and feisty.

"I like the new me, Patrick. Don't you?"

"I do. It's great to hear you're so happy. That's what this trip was all about. But what happened? The last time we talked, you were babbling on about past lives and meeting some guy who looked like the man in your dreams. Did you go see that doctor like you said you would?"

She remembered the late-night house call Dr. O'Donnell had made. "Yeah, I did. He said I was fine. Jet lag on top of a concussion sort of thing. Nothing to worry about."

"Oh, okay. That's good. So, what about the guy? Was he just a figment of your concussive imagination?"

"Afraid not. He's very real and exactly like the man in my dreams—well, save for the Viking apparel and the sword. He's very gentlemanly, a great cook, and he has this perfect little cottage on the beach with a barn and horses. You'd like him."

"You've been to his house?"

"I have," she said, leaving out the part where she slept with him.

"Okay, that's it. I'm coming to Ireland. Sit tight, and

I'll be there in less than twenty-four hours. Do not go back to his house, you hear me?"

Lorraine sat up in a flash. "Patrick, I'm fine."

"I knew I shouldn't have sent you over there by yourself. I regretted the decision the moment your plane lifted off the ground. I should've been there with you. But don't worry, I'll take the next flight out."

She heard him rustling like a madman in the background. "Patrick, put the suitcase back in your closet. You don't need to come to Ireland. I'm fine. Leif's taking very good care of me."

"Taking advantage of you, more like it."

"No, he's not," Lorraine defended. "He'd never do that."

"Right, 'cause after hanging out at his house for two days, you know everything there is to know about him."

"That's right, I do."

"Which is exactly why I'm hauling ass to get to you. You're not thinking clearly, and for all you know, this guy might be a serial killer."

Lorraine laughed at Patrick's exaggeration. Leif might be many things, but he wasn't a serial killer. "You're seriously overreacting."

"So, what if I am." She heard the distinct swift sound of a zipper fasten. "At least I'll know you're safe."

"Patrick, will you stop for a moment and listen to me?" Luggage wheels rolled across his floor as his heavy boots stomped out a definite pace. "Please?" His elongated strides came to a halt, and she held her breath.

"I'm listening," he finally said.

Lorraine breathed a sigh of relief. "Thank you." It felt silly to thank him for lending an ear, but what she had to say next would blow silly out of the water. "Why don't you sit down for this."

"Raine—"

"Please, Patrick? I need you to hear me out and truly listen to me. Don't patronize me like Brad used to do." She must have struck a chord with him. He didn't cut her off or placate her with words she'd want to hear. Instead, she heard the sudden squawk of leather, as if he'd flopped himself down on the living room couch.

"All right, I'm sitting."

Lorraine swallowed. "Do you remember when I asked you about reincarnation?"

"Yeah."

Already, there was a hint of disbelief in Patrick's voice. "Do you believe in it?"

"What does it matter if I believe in it? What does this have to do with you in Ireland?"

"Everything. It has everything to do with it. It's why I've always been drawn to this island. It's why my dreams are filled with unknown places that I should've recognized. It's why the man who haunted my dreams for so long is here, living on Inishmore. It's why I was meant to come here and find him, so we can be together again."

"Again? What do you mean together *again*?"

"I know this may sound off-the-wall, but—" She froze. Patrick might not be ready to hear it. Chances were he'd hang up the phone, catch a red-eye flight to Dublin, and be at her door by morning.

She squeezed her eyes closed, not wanting to sell her best friend short. He was the one person she could depend on, and more times than she could count, he'd sacrificed whatever was necessary to make sure she had someone to lean on. He always went beyond the call of duty when it came to their friendship, and he didn't deserve to be left out in the cold now. Out of everyone she knew, he'd be the one person who'd understand.

She swallowed hard and took a deep breath of courage. "I used to be the daughter of a king in medieval Ireland. I fell in love with a warrior chieftain from Norway. His name was Dægan Ræliksen, and I married him on this very isle at Dún Aonghasa. Then one day, his twin brother came and plundered the isle, leaving my husband for dead. He abducted me to ransom Connacht from my father, but his plan failed. My husband lived, and he gathered an enormous army to track him down. In saving me, he gave his life.

"I watched him die, Patrick. In my arms." Tears spilled from her eyes as she vividly remembered Dægan drawing his last breaths. "We gave him a king's funeral. I'll never forget the sight of that sunset as his longship burned on the horizon. He was gone. My first love ripped from me before we even had a chance to begin our lives together."

"And you think this Leif...guy...is a reincarnated version of your Norse husband?"

"I don't think, Patrick. I know. He says things to me that Dægan has said before—word for word. He bears the mark of a huge battle wound across his thigh, the same one Dægan had. His voice is Dægan's. His kiss is Dægan's. His body is Dægan's. His touch is—"

"Okay, I get it."

Soon after, the awkward silence resumed, and Lorraine couldn't stand it any longer. "You don't believe me, do you?"

Chapter Seventeen

Lorraine swung her legs over the side of the bed, her body tense, her hand cramping from the grip she had on the cell. She loved Patrick, always had, but knowing he didn't believe her hurt worse than anything he could do. This wouldn't be a door between them that had closed with the possibility of one day reopening it. This would be a solid wall, a permanent barrier ultimately dividing them. If he didn't trust what she said was true, there'd be nothing holding them together.

She whispered his name, though it wasn't for getting his attention as much as it was to keep herself from crying. If Patrick didn't believe her, then how could she possibly get Leif to? "Patrick, please say something. Anything?"

His voice finally came over the phone, low and composed. "I'll be frank with you, Raine. It all sounds preposterous. But I do believe you."

Lorraine clutched her chest. "You do?"

"Trust me, I'd rather not. It sounds better if you're the sole crazy one."

An easy laugh escaped her, though she couldn't tell whether he was being truthful or facetious. "So, now what?"

"I don't know," he murmured. She could picture him sinking low into the couch and stretching his long legs out—what he always did when he needed to think. "Have you told him?"

Lorraine imagined Leif repudiating her on the spot. "I'm afraid to. He's not as credulous as you are."

"Thanks a lot," he said solemnly.

"I mean, he's not likely to believe a word of it unless he can back it up with scientific evidence. He's an archeologist. I'll need more than just a birthmark and a few analogous conversations to convince him."

"So, find something."

"What do you mean?"

"I don't know, you used to live there. In the time you were together, was there a special place you used to frequent? Or anything said that only you and he would know about?" He scoffed. "This sounds so bizarre. Me asking you about places and things from a time period hundreds of years before my birth."

"I know. And I can't tell you how much it means to me to have your support, Patrick. Most people would think I'm strung out on hallucinogens."

"I won't lie. I'm still tossing around that idea," he joked. "But it's you. I know you'd never lie. If you say you've had a past life with a man you're presently...involved with...then I've no choice but to help you help him remember. That is what you want, right?"

Patrick's words eased her nervousness, and the burden of carrying this remarkable discovery on her shoulders alone had lifted. "Yes, I want Leif to remember me as the woman he came upon by the River Shannon, who enchanted him so much, he couldn't live without her. The woman he took as his wife. The woman he fell madly in love with."

"How did you know he was in love with you?"

A smile automatically curled Lorraine's lips. "I felt it. I

felt it in everything he did. In the heat of his eyes as he looked at me. In his embrace as he held me tight. In the poetic words he used to express his heart's desire. He once gave me a gift. A king's chest of immeasurable value, and it was then that I knew he loved me." She drifted off to the day Dægan had given it to her.

Dægan took my hand in his before he spoke. "I know this may seem sudden and a bit forward, but I want to give you a gift—one that would seem more fitting had I had a chance to offer your father a sufficient bride price."

He studied me, holding fast to the innocence of my face. Like a child, my eyes sparkled with anticipation. He began with a story.

"There once was a king blessed with power, wealth, and dignity. He fell in love with a woman, and she loved him…"

Lorraine stood from the bed and walked to the window. What she wouldn't give to see that chest again. Back in the day, she knew it meant the world to Dægan. She couldn't help but think that if Leif could see it now, he'd have to remember giving it to her. But who knows if it survived after more than a thousand years, and who knew where the chest ended up after her death.

She shrugged off the idea of the chest and leaned her hip against the wall. With the cell pressed to her ear, she stood gazing out the window. From her cottage, she had a spectacular view of the island's beach, with Leif's house and barn nestled in picturesque charm between the rocky shoreline and the grassy fields. His horses grazed within the lush green pastures, fenced by ancient dry stone walls, while purple and yellow flowers sprinkled the grass with color.

As she took in the beautiful scenery of today, a bygone image slowly emerged before her eyes. Where horses grazed, cows and sheep dotted the fields. Where the ocean lapped the shore, dragon-prowed longships lined the banks. And where Leif's homestead existed, a community of longhouses replaced it.

She gripped the sill, leaning in for a closer look. "What are the chances…" she muttered under her breath.

"What's wrong?"

She heard the stark concern in Patrick's voice. "Nothing's wrong. In fact, everything is just perfect. Like it was meant to be."

"You're not making any sense, Raine."

Normally, his stern voice would've curtailed her excitement, but in envisioning the Norse settlement from when she'd lived in the tenth century, she was about ready to leap out of her shoes. "Patrick, you're not going to believe this."

"Oh, I don't know. I can't imagine you trumping the reincarnation card with something more outrageous?"

"How about Leif's cottage sitting atop Dægan's longhouse?" she challenged. "If I remember correctly, it might have been rotated a bit, but I'm almost sure of its placement. What if…" The words dangled on the edge of her tongue. The likelihood of anything still existing after all that time was slim to none. "Do you think something could have been left behind?"

"You mean like an artifact from your king's chest? Or a piece of the carved wood buried beneath his home?"

"Well, yeah. What's so funny about that? Artifacts are found every day in lots of ordinary places, somewhere one would least expect. Leif's an archeologist. Maybe that's why he's here in the first place. Maybe he's drawn to this place like I was and needs my assistance to unearth the locations of—"

"Raine, you're reaching."

"I am not."

"You are."

Her spirits plummeted. "Maybe I am."

"Look, you can't go snooping around the guy's house looking for buried treasure. He'll drop you like a hot potato. Can't you just get him to fall in love with you naturally, and be happy with that? So what if he doesn't recognize you from his past? You'd still have him in your life."

"But—"

"No one is going to believe you like I do, Raine. If you try to convince him he's your long-lost husband from the Viking age, he's likely to think you're off your rocker. And he'll want nothing to do with you. Is making him remember things he's doubtful to recollect in the first place worth losing him?"

The sharp pain of that dreadful scenario pierced her heart. The last thing she wanted to do was lose Leif. It would be like losing him in death all over again.

Chapter Eighteen

Six hours later, Lorraine sat aboard a horse-drawn carriage, leaving the bustling island village of Kilronan and heading back to Leif's house with a bag full of groceries, a bottle of wine, and a present she'd bought in one of the tourist gift shops along the street.

The wind had picked up and the sky grew dark on the scenic trek along the upper road. She pulled up the collar of her brand-new and authentic Aran Isle sweater and tucked her nose down inside. The tightly woven cream-colored wool served as a great insulator beneath her coat, but it wasn't what had sold her on the garment. The selling point had been the unique vertical hand-stitched patterns characteristic of the Aran-style stitching, each one as exceptional as the next. She liked them so much, she bought several, one for herself, one for Patrick, and one for Leif.

"Are you certain you've sent me to the right address, *a mhuirnín*? This'd be the home of Mr. Dæganssen...and his brother."

Lorraine looked up, detecting some disdain in the driver's voice. "Aye, it is, Mr. Flanagan."

He pulled the cart to a gentle stop and eyed her inquisitively, specifically her dark hair. "Are ye family, then?"

She smiled warmly. "Nah, I'm just a friend."

He glanced at the bottle of wine sticking out of her

bag. "Friends bring whiskey to a gathering. Lovers bring wine."

She gathered her belongings and stepped off the carriage. "Interesting theory, Mr. Flanagan. I'll have to keep that in mind the next time I attend a party."

"Two people isn't a party, though. It's an engagement of the heart conducive to intimacy."

"Well, I'll be." A familiar voice broke in behind Lorraine. "Paddy Flanagan not only steals my clients out from under me with cunning, but it seems he blows intellectual smoke up their arses at no extra charge as well."

Lorraine whirled around to see Kristoff coming out of the barn. A wry smile tested his lips as he wiped his hands on a dirty, paint-stained rag.

"Kristoff," Mr. Flanagan muttered with gross contempt. "It's not considered thievery if the competition has taken the day off."

"I'm painting my carriage," Kristoff defended. "When it's finished, it will look a whole lot better than this splinter box on wheels you've got hitched behind that nag."

"You can put silk on a goat, but it's still a goat," Mr. Flanagan argued back. He rapped the reins once, and his horse eased into an ambling gait. He kindly tipped his hat at Lorraine and said, "May you have the hindsight to know where you've been, the foresight to know where you're going, and the insight to know when you're going too far. *Slán go foill, a mhuirnín.*"

"*Slán, a Flanagan a chara,*" she called after him. "*Is go raibh maith agat!*" By the time she turned around, Kristoff was already at her side taking the grocery bag from her. He smelled of fresh paint and turpentine, lending proof that he was, indeed, painting something.

"Here, let me carry that for you." When he peeked

inside her bag, his face brightened. "What are we cooking tonight?"

"Parmesan-crusted chicken," she said, glancing back at Mr. Flanagan as they climbed the steps to Leif's porch. "So, what was all that about?"

"Nothing but a little friendly rivalry. Paddy and I go way back." Though she never asked, Kristoff explained how he and Mr. Flanagan first met in a Dublin pub during the World Cup finals where his team beat Ireland in an upset match. "Four years later, we met again, only this time the upset was over a woman."

"Who was the victor in that bout?"

Kristoff tilted his head and frowned before opening the door for her. "Did you really think I'd lose?"

Lorraine had to laugh at his arrogance. "You know, good looks aren't as important to a woman as you might think."

"Tell that to Paddy." He leaned in close and whispered, "His girlfriend went home with me that night. I don't think he'd agree with you."

"You stole his girlfriend?" Lorraine asked as they walked together toward the kitchen. Kristoff set the bag of groceries on the table and pulled out the wine, eyeing the label. "She was gagging for it. But blimey O'Reilly, that redhead had a set of lungs on her. On *multiple occasions*, I thought the windows would shatter."

Lorraine rolled her eyes at Kristoff's emphasis on two specific words, as if he felt inclined to disclose the sordid details of their sexual encounter. "It's a wonder how Flanagan hasn't hired a hit man for you by now."

"He wouldn't do that," Kristoff said, handing her the bottle. "He still owes me."

"Owes you for what?"

"For roughing up a few bevvied tourists who tried to stiff him after he'd carted them around all day. Flanagan was about to consume a knuckle Reuben when I showed up."

"I didn't know you had it in you, Kristoff."

"Well, it was three against one. I had to even it up a little bit. Besides, no one picks on Flanagan but me."

"Is that why you came out of the barn, instead of Leif?"

"Lucky for you I did. Flanagan was pulling out all the stops with that poetic Irish codswallop. He would've blithered on and on."

She put the wine in the refrigerator and narrowed her gaze. "Let me guess. The fiery redhead preferred the poetic codswallop and went running back to Flanagan."

Every muscle in Kristoff's face clenched. "That was the word around town, but who knows for sure."

Lorraine burst out laughing, then, when she realized she was the only one, she lowered the enthusiasm to a quiet chuckle. Kristoff might have appeared to be the vain self-absorbed womanizer on the outside, but inside, he had feelings. It was obvious the fickle redhead had left behind some damage. "Sounds like she doesn't know what she wants."

Kristoff shrugged.

"Do you really want to waste your energy on a woman who's that indecisive? I'd think your type of woman has strength in her character, and she'd need to be confident with herself in order to keep up with you. Besides, a good set of lungs is overrated."

Kristoff seemed to enjoy her joke. It was the first time she'd ever witnessed his humble side, and she hoped he'd bring it out more often. "I should get back to the barn." He thumbed over his shoulder. "Leif's probably thinking I'm hitting on you by now."

"Thanks for helping me carry all this stuff."

"You're welcome." His smile was kind, as if he truly enjoyed assisting her and didn't have a hidden agenda behind the gentlemanly demeanor.

"Hey, why don't you stay with us for dinner?" Lorraine suggested as she unloaded the rest of the bag. "I know I'll have plenty, that is if you like Italian."

He fidgeted nervously. "I love Italian. And I appreciate the offer, but I think I'll pass. I may not be as poetically versed as ol' Flanagan out there, but I have a clever saying I often refer to at moments like these."

"Oh?" Lorraine said, her interest piqued. "What's that?"

"Three's a crowd." He winked with a smile. As he turned to leave, he added, "I'll let Leif know you're here."

"Actually," she called out, "I'm a bit early, and I'd like to take the extra time to cook the meal and get ready." She reached into her backpack and revealed a little black dress by its spaghetti strap, biting her lip as she displayed her plans.

Kristoff nodded in understanding. "I see." The smile he boasted eventually faded into a concerned look. "Can I ask you something?"

Lorraine was almost afraid of his open-ended question. She let the dress fall back into its hiding place and crossed her arms. "Sure."

"You're here for two weeks on holiday, correct?"

"Yes…"

"And after that, you're heading back to the States."

Honestly, she hadn't thought that far in advance. She didn't want to return to Kentucky once her vacation was over in hopes she'd have made some headway with Leif, and she figured she'd cross that bridge when she got there. Given the exceptional circumstances of her blossoming relationship with Leif, it was best to let Kristoff believe she didn't have ulterior motives. "My flight leaves in ten days."

"Ten days," he repeated. "And what are your plans in those ten days?"

"I'm not sure what you mean." Lorraine knew exactly what he meant, but for the sake of borrowing time, she wanted to hear it straight from his mouth.

"I mean, what are your plans with my brother?" He casually rapped his knuckles on the kitchen table. "I don't know if you've noticed or not, but Leif is into you. Seriously into you. No woman has ever been able to…" he struggled to find the word, "…*interest* him. He's not the kind of man who falls easily. This is the happiest I've ever seen him, and I thank you for coming along when you did. Sometimes, I think he's too wrapped up in his work. He's got some excessive need to find out about his ancestors. To find out who *he* is. It's like he's not satisfied with just being Leif Dæganssen, son of Lars and Ingeborg of Trondheim. But with you stepping into his life all of a sudden, those obsessive ambitions have all gone to the wayside. At least for the moment anyway. You've given him something else to focus on.

"That being said, he is my brother, and I don't want to see him get hurt. Trust me, I'm all for noncommittal relationships and fly-by-night promiscuous affairs. But that's not Leif. If you plan to live it up with him like your American spring flings in tropical paradises, perhaps you should find someone else."

Lorraine found it difficult to face Kristoff. It pained her to know he thought so little of her, yet at the same time, she understood exactly where he was coming from. She had no intention of "living it up" with Leif and leaving him behind like a typical run-of-the-mill college fling. He meant too much to her. But how did one convey a deep sense of adoration and respect for a man she'd met only a few days ago without sounding like a desperate female on the hunt? "I can't predict the future, Kristoff, nor can I say where Leif and I will be at the end of my ten days, but I can assure you I have no intention of hurting your brother. I suppose I should admit I'm falling for him too, though I'm not sure it helps matters."

Kristoff gave a little chuckle. "That's cute."

Lorraine looked at him, puzzled. "What is?"

"Leif is falling…and so is Raine."

The play on words had Lorraine laughing with him. "I never thought of it that way."

"All right," Kristoff said, backing out of the kitchen. "Enough of this. I'll go back to the barn with Leif and pretend you're not here. I assume you'll be making an entrance?" he asked, gesturing toward the dress in the bag.

She bit her lip again. "If I must."

"I think he'd like that. Besides, I'd like you to see the project we're working on. Trust me, you've never seen a boat quite like this."

Lorraine smiled, accepting Kristoff's candid invitation. "When dinner's finished, I'll come a calling."

Kristoff hesitated at the kitchen doorway, gripping its frame. "If you don't mind, I'd like this conversation to remain here, between us. Leif would be sorely pissed if he knew I intervened."

"Of course," she agreed. He nodded once and then he was gone.

****

"About time you came back," Leif said from behind the hull of the boat once Kristoff entered the barn.

"A man's got to take a leak sometimes. And since when are you timing me?"

"Since they've become half-hour intervals. Seriously, what the hell took you so long?"

Kristoff snatched the rag from his shoulder and threw it at his brother. "I've been blessed with a huge bladder. It's equivalent to the other sizeable components of my lower half."

Leif rolled his eyes and discarded the rag. "Spare me."

"You asked."

Leif stood with his hands on his hips, eyeing the two wooden objects in his spacious barn. To his left stood a newly painted horse carriage complete with a shiny black leather driving harness. To his right, a rough replica of a hand-hewed Viking longship in serious need of a good sanding. "We got a lot done. I'd say in a few more days, we could have this baby seaworthy."

Kristoff touched the side of the ship and ran his hand along its gunwale like it was a desirable mistress. "She's going to be beautiful."

Leif couldn't argue. Though he hated the long, painstaking hours spent hand-hewing the planks as his Norse ancestors did and attaching them to the keel with wooden dowels and iron rivets, the product of their year-long undertaking was emerging into a remarkable work of art. "That she is."

"Think we can finish the sanding tonight?" Kristoff asked eagerly.

"Well, if you don't run off on another pissing intermission, I'd say we could. But no matter what, I'm quitting at seven. Raine's making dinner tonight."

"She is, huh?"

Leif eyed his brother, disturbed by the coyness of his grin. "Yeah, she is. And that means you need to make yourself scarce—even if she invites you to stay."

Kristoff picked up a roll of sandpaper. He tossed it up in the air and caught it a few times before goading Leif. "What if she's adamant? I don't want to be rude."

Leif reached out and caught the roll mid-juggle. "It never stopped you before, and tonight isn't the night. Understand?"

"Yeah, I get it. You want her all to yourself."

Leif ignored him and adhered the sandpaper disc to a manual palm sander he grabbed from the shelf. "Do you blame me?"

"Are you asking for *my* approval?" Kristoff asked sarcastically.

Leif leapt over the side of the boat and squatted inside the hull, beginning to sand with long, methodical strokes. "Maybe not exactly your approval, but I'd like to know you respect how I feel about her."

"And how *do* you feel about her?"

"As crazy as it sounds, I feel like I've known her all my life. And I don't want to stop getting to know her. I want to know all there is to know about Lorraine O'Connor."

"Before she leaves, you mean," Kristoff added.

Knowing her visit to Ireland was temporary hit home. "What if I don't want her to leave?"

"Then don't let her."

Leif shook the idea from his head. "She has a life in the States. Family. Friends."

"Everyone's got that, Leif. Question is, is it enough to keep her there? More importantly, what's to keep her here? Would that be you?"

"I'd like to think so." Leif went back to his sanding and ruminated over how she'd react if he approached her with the idea of staying in Ireland. "She'd probably laugh at me," he said. "Listen to me. I sound like a love-crazed teen."

"*Are* you in love with her?"

Leif's hand halted mid-sand. "Is that even possible?"

"You're asking the wrong person about love, pal. But if you're asking me if she's worth holding on to? Then yeah, I think you'd be a fool to let her slip through your hands."

Chapter Nineteen

Lorraine checked herself one last time in the mirror of Leif's bathroom. She'd darkened her eye shadow to a smoky gray and dramatized her lashes with a deep black mascara to call attention to one of her best assets: her eyes. She was pleased that they were the first things she noticed, and hoped they would be the first things Leif would notice as well.

Fluffing her long dark hair, she smiled at the transformation she'd made. In the past days, Leif had only seen her natural country-girl look. Tonight, she wanted to show him her sexy glamorous side, with a backless black dress and a whole lot of leg.

Content with her appearance, she exited the bathroom with a skip. Her high heels clicked confidently across the floor as she returned to the kitchen and checked the chicken in the oven. After she lit a few taper candles she'd picked up in Kilronan, she glanced across the elegant place settings on the table and the wine chilling in the ice bucket. Satisfied with her efforts, she turned and strode out the door, her heart leaping for the night ahead.

As she descended the porch steps, she started to have second thoughts about making that entrance Kristoff had talked about. There was something unsettling about knowing both brothers would be analyzing her from top to bottom. It wasn't so much Leif's opinion that shook her nerves, but Kristoff's. What if he determined she wasn't worthy of his brother? What if she didn't live up to Kristoff's expectations?

She pushed her ridiculous fretting aside. This night wasn't about Kristoff. It was about spending as much time with Leif as he'd allow, and hoping the connection he said he felt was enough to bind them together.

Smoothing her skirt down her legs and drawing in a long deep breath of sea-salt air, she entered the barn and froze. To her left, warm light filtered through the slats of a room adjacent the barn stalls, and the dragon-headed prow from an impressive Viking longship stood proud within it. Even more stunning was the sight of Leif's bare chest and shoulders glistening with sweat and sawdust.

He had no idea she stood there. She admired the muscles of his arms flexing as he glided sandpaper up and down the inner planks of the ship. For a few stolen moments, she watched him and listened to his voice resonate within the walls of the barn as he talked and joked with his brother. It didn't matter what he was saying, just that she could see him in his element.

Laughter erupted between the brothers, and it shook her from her stupor. Her ankle twisted and knocked her off balance, sending her into the wall. Leif looked up at the noise, and they locked eyes.

His body stilled and his Adam's apple bobbed as he swallowed. His gaze drifted slowly downward, and he took in her appearance inch by inch. She could almost feel the intensity of his inspection blazing a trail over her entire body.

She started to walk toward him, but her ankles wobbled again. Before she might have hit the ground, Leif leapt from the hull and caught her, his eyes still drinking her in.

"Hi."

Lorraine smiled at the simplicity of his words, though she knew it meant so much more. The huskiness of his voice deceived the casualness he tried to fake.

"You look…"

"Sexy as hell," Kristoff said as he popped up from behind the ship. Leif turned and glared at him. "What? Like you weren't thinking it?"

Leif turned his attention back to her. "You'll have to excuse him. He loses his manners when a stunning woman enters the room."

Lorraine gobbled up his compliment. "Thank you."

Leif stepped back, still holding fast to her hands as he took another thorough look. "How did you get this dress past airport security?"

Lorraine giggled. "This old thing?"

He started to pull her close but stopped himself. Glancing down at his sweaty body, he frowned. "I need a shower."

"A cold one," Kristoff jibed. "In the meantime, Lorraine, get a load of this." Kristoff gestured with outstretched arms. "Isn't my longship a beauty?"

Leif stepped aside and escorted her forward. She felt the slight pressure of his hand on the bare skin of her lower back as she walked, and although he meant to assure her footing, he made it doubly difficult for her to walk with poise.

As she approached the streamlined, handcrafted vessel, the smell of oak wood infused her senses. Looking up at the carved dragon head looming above her, she recalled the first time she had seen Dægan's longship in Limerick's port.

Through the fog, I saw the large wooden prow of Dægan's drakkar. It was carved as an openmouthed dragon with teeth and scales, raising its head proudly for all to see, even in the dead of night. Its fiendish, bulging eyes stared at everyone who walked in and out of its hull. The neck was rigid and self-righteous, long and curved as it preceded the rest of the ship and ended with a coiled tail for the sternpost.

As we pushed closer, I discerned the rest of the wicked ship's body through the murky fog. Colorfully painted round shields arrayed along the gunwales, each one as striking as the next. Five oars on each side extended into the river like a spindle-legged spider, while the belly brimmed with chests, barrels, and assorted sacks.

The impressive boat provoked a feeling of instinctive fear in my heart. I gathered that the Northmen had built it with that very purpose in mind when landing on virgin soil.

Though the dragon-headed prow of this longship was just as menacing as Dægan's, the familiar likeness warmed her. Leif skirted around her and smiled. "You built this?" she asked, still in awe of how closely it resembled the real thing.

"I built this," Kristoff corrected. "I just used Leif for the manual labor."

"It's true," Leif admitted. "He's the expert designer. The only thing I'll ever give him due credit for in this lifetime."

Lorraine looked at Kristoff with pride. "I'm amazed. Speechless. When you told me to come out and see your boat, I had no idea it was—"

"Wait," Leif interrupted, looking between the two of them. Settling on his brother, he pointed. "You knew she was here?"

Kristoff slapped his hands together. "And that's my cue." As he rounded the prow, he waved good-bye to Lorraine. "Enjoy your evening."

Lorraine looked at Leif now, realizing by the astonished look on his face she'd blown her own cover.

"You were in cahoots with him this whole time?" Leif joked. She bit her lip, and he removed an imaginary knife from his back. "Don't tell me Kristoff saw that dress before I did."

"In his defense, it wasn't on me when he saw it."

Leif slumped against the side of the ship for theatrical purposes. "I can't believe this. Betrayed by the only woman I care about."

His words echoed in her ears. "You care about me?"

He held out his hand to her, and she accepted it. He stroked his thumb over the tops of her knuckles as he gazed into her eyes. "I feel like I can't remember a time when I didn't care about you. It's as though my life, before we met, doesn't exist."

His outspoken confession held her fixed to the floor, and she found it hard to breathe. He tugged her closer so she stood between his thighs.

"Much of my life has been spent soul-searching and trying to discover my ancestors in hopes of finding my place in this world. For as long as I can remember, I've been looking for something that, in the grand scheme of things, has no bearing on who I am at all. I never realized that until I met you.

"When I look in your eyes, I see myself the way I'd want to see me: a content man ready to make a leap of faith. As far as I'm concerned, it doesn't matter where I came from or how I'm linked to those who came before me. In my heart, I feel as if I've finally found the one answer to all my questions." He paused and reached up to brush the back of his hand across her cheek. The distinct smell of lumber and Leif's heady scent swirled around her. "My journey's end begins with you, Raine."

Lorraine felt as if someone had jerked the carpet out from underneath her. Her knees shook and her stomach fluttered as if she'd trapped a thousand butterflies. She gripped his arms for support without knowing, and tried like the devil to regain some sense of composure.

"I apologize for putting you on the spot," he said. "Perhaps, I've said things I shouldn't have. But something inside me tells me that you understand completely. Am I a fool for thinking such things?"

"You're not," she stammered. She wanted to tell him why he'd felt so connected in a way that defied normal human emotion. She was dying to profess their existence as past lovers and tell him that they'd somehow gotten a second chance to be together in this life. But she held her tongue.

"I do understand how you feel. I feel it too. I wanted to tell you, but I was afraid."

Leif caught her chin with his warm, gentle hand, and the sharp angles of his face smoothed in sympathy. "It's only to be expected. You were with a man who took advantage of everything you'd given. He broke your heart."

Lorraine let Leif believe that her fear came from Brad's infidelity. It was better that way. For now.

"I can't say what lies ahead for us," he added. "But I promise I'll always be honest with you. And I'll never do anything to hurt you." He slid his hand around the back of her neck and wove his fingers into her hair, pulling her toward his lips. "I will never hurt you, Raine. Ever."

The words he repeated brushed across her lips like lustrous silk. She closed her eyes, and their lips met. Everything around her ceased to exist, save for the man she'd always dreamed of. The man she'd always loved.

Chapter Twenty

As soon as Lorraine heard the water from Leif's shower turn on, she dove into her backpack and pulled out her cell. She couldn't wait to tell Patrick the good news.

Counting the rings, he finally picked up on the third. "Hello?"

"You're not going to believe this."

His laughed echoed through the receiver. "Try me."

"I think Leif's falling in love with me."

"You *think*?"

"Well, he didn't come out and say it, but he said his journey's end begins with me. With me, Patrick. He said *with me*."

"He told you this?"

"He did," she said, glancing at the candle-lit table behind her. "And I've made him dinner tonight, so I think the rest of the night is going to be even better."

"Where is he now?"

"In the shower. Why?"

"I'm wondering why you're calling me if he's there with you."

"Because you're my best friend. You're always the first person I'm dying to call when something amazing happens."

"You seem very happy, Raine."

"Oh, you have no idea," she exclaimed, pacing beside the table. "I can't believe I'm getting a second chance to be with him, to be with the man I was once married to. It's like a fairy tale. Oh, Patrick, talking me into going to Ireland was the best idea ever, and I thank you for being so adamant. I mean, what if I'd refused to go? What if I hadn't taken your advice about staying on Inishmore and I'd booked a hotel in Dublin? I never would have found him."

"Yeah, it's pretty amazing how things have worked out. I'm still trying to wrap my head around it."

Patrick's tone sounded rather subdued, and she tried to decipher the meaning behind his words. "I know you're having a hard time with this. And I don't blame you."

"Blame me for what?"

"For second-guessing me."

"It's not that," Patrick said. "It's just that it's not like you to be this happy. You've never been this way over a guy before."

"This isn't just any guy, Patrick. This is Dægan, son of Rælik. My Norse warrior and chieftain husband has been reborn in the body of Leif Dæganssen, a present-day archeologist who digs up castle ruins and the grave sites of historical icons."

"That's an impressive set of credentials. Hard to argue when you introduce him that way."

"Patrick, I'm serious."

"Well, you have to admit, it's pretty bizarre, you remembering a past life and all. You have to give me some time to accept it."

"Right."

"So, is Leif aware of his previous status? Does he remember you as you remember him?"

"If he has, he doesn't let on."

"You sound disappointed."

"Maybe a little. But you know, I've given some serious thought to what you said this morning, and I think you're right. Making Leif remember who he was isn't as important as keeping him in my life. He may *never* remember who he used to be, and if I force it on him, I could lose him. I can't stand the thought of that happening." She shifted her weight to one hip and sighed, ready to change the subject. "Anyway... How's Kentucky? Does Captain even know I'm gone?"

"Oh, it's pitiful," Patrick said. "He's been lying at the foot of your bed since you left, looking at me like I kicked you out of the house. It's ridiculous."

Lorraine had to laugh. Patrick had bought Captain for himself, but the dog had taken to her like a savory beef-flavored bone the day she moved in. "Scratch him behind the ears for me, will you?"

"Yeah, whatever."

Lorraine put an ear toward the hall, listening for the shower. Still running. "You got big plans this Friday?"

Patrick hummed in thought before he came clean. "Beth's coming over for the weekend."

"All weekend?"

"Mm-hm."

"I bet she loved the idea of me being in Ireland."

"She did."

"You don't sound so excited. I thought you liked her."

"I do like her. She's a great girl. But...she's not..."

"Patrick, I'm sorry. Leif's getting out of the shower. I gotta go. I'll call you tomorrow."

****

Leif leaned back in his chair, setting his fork beside his

clean plate, and wiped his mouth with his napkin. He sat there, eyes fixed on hers, as if contemplating his next words. "I've never had a woman cook for me before. I can certainly get used to this."

"Does that mean I have better culinary skills than Kristoff?"

"That and so much more. Honestly, this has got to be the best meal I've ever eaten."

"You know," Lorraine said, standing up from the table and drawing near. "You don't have to flatter me. Regardless of what you think of my cooking, I'll let you get into this dress."

"Is that so?" He reached for her wrist and pulled her onto his lap. The heat from his body radiated through her thin evening attire, and she wrapped her arms around his neck, relishing how great it felt to be with him. "The night is still young, you know, and the moon is bright," she proposed, twirling the hair at his neck. "We could go for a walk along the shore if you wanted."

He tucked his nose in the crevice of her throat and breathed in. "I'll do whatever you want."

Lorraine closed her eyes and let his mouth roam up and down her neck. If she kept this up, they wouldn't go anywhere. Shivers climbed up her spine, and she giggled, trying her best to resist him. She put her hands on his chest and pushed. "Good things come to those who wait, Leif."

He clenched his teeth and glanced down at his lap. "Tell that to him."

Lorraine smiled, amazed at how easily Leif's body responded to her. But Leif proved he still had willpower and stood with her in his arms. Setting her gently on her feet, he cast another glance over her body as he twirled her once.

He clicked his tongue a few times. "It's a shame you can't wear those heels on our moonlight walk. You're liable to snap your ankle on the rocks, and then I'd have to call Dr. O'Donnell again." He looked as though he were contemplating the risk, and that getting cursed in Gaelic by O'Donnell's wife might be worth leaving the heels on. "Nah, you shouldn't. His wife would beat me over the head with a cast iron skillet."

"Not to mention the pain I'd be in breaking my ankle," she said jokingly, emphasizing what he should've thought was more important.

He smiled. "Of course. But you're putting them back on later."

"I guess that can be arranged," she said, slipping them off. Now three inches shorter, she felt so small standing next to him, especially when he reached around her and filled their wineglasses.

He did so with the talent of a debonair waiter and kicked off his own shoes, offering his elbow. "Shall we?"

She took her glass from him and slipped her arm through his. As she leaned into his rock-solid physique for comfort, they left the house arm in arm and walked to the shoreline of the beach. The sibilant sound of breaking waves filled the air, and Lorraine was the happiest she'd ever been in the ambience of the starlit night. Being with Leif was a dream come true.

"Careful," he warned as they strolled over the pebble-strewn beach. His arm flexed around hers in a vise until they reached the lapping waves. The shock of the cold water rushing over her ankles caused her to gasp and tiptoe, but he swept her into his arms and carried her to a large bolder.

"So much for long walks on the beach," he teased, sitting beside her.

"I'm used to warm, equatorial waters and sunbaked sand."

"You'll not find that here." He tipped his glass to his mouth and added, "This is Ireland. You're lucky the moon is out."

Lorraine took a sip of her wine, or rather some liquid courage. "I'm lucky I'm with you."

Leif turned to face her and clinked his glass with hers. "To small blessings."

As she drank to the toast, she stared at him. At an impressive six foot three, with the sharp angles of his profile cutting into the blackness of the night and his soft hair blowing in the wind, he was the perfect picture of male excellence.

"Did you get in touch with your friend?" he asked, interrupting her thoughts.

"W-what?"

"Your friend in the States...Patrick? Did you reach him?"

"Oh yes. Yes, of course. I talked to him this morning before I went into Kilronan."

"Was he upset that he couldn't get in touch with you?"

She steered her brain from Leif's gorgeous body into this unexpected conversation. "No, he was just worried."

"Did you tell him why you hadn't called?"

"I told him about you, if that's what you're hinting."

He flashed a smile that sparkled in his eyes. "I'm betting he wants to jump on the next plane and kick my ass, doesn't he?"

"Maybe."

Self-satisfied laughter erupted from deep within him, and he chased it down with the last gulp of his wine. "I used to know a Patrick. I met him a few years ago at a horse auction in Galway. I'd bought Thor and needed a set of shoes put on before I made the trip back. He was one of the farriers there. Can't recall his last name, though, and probably wouldn't know it if you said it."

Lorraine's eyes widened. "A farrier? My friend Patrick's a farrier too."

"Has he been to Ireland?"

Lorraine thought for a second. "He's been here many times, working the races mostly. The Irish Grand National, the Curragh Derby, the Killarney Festival. And those are just the ones I can remember. He was always traveling."

"Was?" Leif baited.

She shivered as the night air crept under her skin. "Was until my parents died." She watched as Leif unfastened his shirt and was distracted when he revealed his muscled chest one button at a time. It didn't matter how many times she saw him shirtless. Each time rendered her keyed up and flustered. "H-he took me...um...under his wing and..."

"Watched over you?"

The fabric was still warm from his body heat when he wrapped it around her shoulders, and she was most grateful. "Yes, you could say that. He's been the protective big brother I've never had. Most people don't understand our relationship. They think that because two people of the opposite sex are living together under the same roof, they should be romantically involved."

"No, I get it," Leif assured her. "Though I hate to admit it, I guess that's who Kristoff is for me. A protective brother. 'Course, I'd have no qualms about trading him in for someone else."

"You don't mean that."

"Oh, I do," Leif insisted as he tightened the shirt around her neck. "Kristoff is like…"

Lorraine recalled the discussion she and Dægan had had about his brother, Eirik, centuries ago. "Let me guess. He's like the runt of the litter you know you shouldn't keep, but you do anyway, hoping he'll be worth something someday."

Leif grinned from ear to ear. "You know Kristoff well, then."

"I think I know *you* well enough to know what you think of him."

He angled his body toward hers. "What am I thinking right now?"

Her mouth went dry at the sudden passion blazing in his eyes. He didn't give her time to guess and scooped her up in arms, kissing her all the way to the house.

Chapter Twenty-one

Leif shut the door to his guest room. Lorraine's heels dangled from the hook of his fingers as he watched her disrobe from the shirt he'd given her. The black dress she wore clung snugly to her hips, alluding to the womanly curves she possessed, and he couldn't wait to get her out of it.

He stepped toward her and presented the sexy shoes. "If you don't mind." His voice came out strained, a lot more than he cared to demonstrate.

She smiled and held on to his forearm as she steadied herself one foot at a time to slip them on. Though her touch was innocent, it sent a bolt of electricity through his body.

With a flick of his wrist, he seized her and wrenched her closer. A sweet whimper of surprise resounded from her luscious mouth. He kissed her lips hard this time and tangled his hands in her hair. The sugary taste of wine mixed with the wicked flavor of her own desire spurred an unruly sense of greed in him. Realizing he was too rough and might be hurting her, he pushed out of the kiss and backed away.

"I'm sorry. I don't know what came over me," he confessed. "It's as if every aggression I've ever felt and every emotion I've ever kept hidden are threatening to unleash. I don't know where it's coming from, Raine."

Lorraine stared at him, silent as the grave.

"I know you don't understand what I'm saying, and I know we've only met a few days ago," he tried to explain. "But everything inside me, down to the bare fundamentals of my makeup, tells me I've known you all my life."

"Even before you were born."

Her thin, shaky voice conveyed a statement rather than a question. "Yes," he said excitedly. "Like you and I were…"

"Destined?"

"How can this be making sense to you?"

Lorraine's face lit up in a twinkling smile. "I've felt it too. From the moment I saw you. And with each passing day, it's grown. But I never wanted to tell you for fear you'd…"

He rushed toward her and wrapped his arms around her. "I don't know what this is," he said, placing his hand over her heart, then over his. "But I don't want to imagine myself without it. Without you. I need you."

Lorraine hugged him tight and burrowed into his chest. "I'm here, Leif. I'm not going anywhere."

****

Lorraine's heavy lids fluttered open, and she felt Leif's warm, hard body spooned against her back. He'd fallen asleep with his arm protectively draped around her, and she'd never felt more secure. The imminent approach of her last days in Ireland didn't scare her because she'd connected with Leif on a level that wouldn't allow him to even think of parting ways. She was confident she'd wrapped herself tightly enough around his heart that he wouldn't let go.

Snuggling closer, she felt him stir, and a long, contented sigh tickled the back of her neck. "Are you awake?" she whispered.

"I am." He pulled her tighter against him. "But I think I'm still dreaming. Or I've died and gone to heaven."

Leif's sleepy words coated her like hot fudge. Being with him was better than opening presents on Christmas morning. But then she stiffened, remembering the gift she'd meant to give him last night, and he felt it.

"What's wrong?" he asked drowsily.

"I forgot to give you your present."

"Present? For what?" he mumbled.

She spun in his arms and faced him with a huge smile. "Your birthday, silly. Which brings me to ask, what *is* the actual date of your birth? Surely by now I've earned the right to know."

A quiet chuckle sounded in his chest. "You've earned that a long time ago. Along with any other secret I have."

She toyed with his hair, twirling it around her finger. "You have secrets?"

"Doesn't everyone?"

His question ricocheted in her head. If she denied it, she'd be lying. If she concurred, he was liable to ask about hers. And as much as she'd loved to get her secret off her chest, she didn't think he was ready to know it. "Only if they choose to have them," she stated vaguely.

Leif sat up on his elbow. "Then what if I told you I have one?"

Unable to fathom what kind of secret Leif had kept to himself, she braced herself for something big. "Then I'd say your secret is safe with me."

He flashed a bright smile. "You first."

Her heart stopped. "W-what?"

"You first," he repeated. "Hand over the present, and I'll let you in on my little secret. Deal?"

Relief washed over her. "Wait here, I'll be right back." Hijacking the sheet from the bed, she gathered it around her and padded out of the room.

Lorraine returned, carrying two beautifully wrapped boxes of different sizes. Leif sat on the edge of the bed, wearing his pants from last night and waiting patiently. He loved surprises and couldn't begin to guess what she'd gotten him.

She plopped down next to him, wrapped in her sheet cocoon, and handed him the larger of the two boxes. "It's not much, but I wanted to get it for you." As he tore open the wrapping, she quickly added, "I have one too."

Parting the tissue paper, he saw the woven designs of a recognizable sweater, unique to the island. "Oh wow, an Aran sweater," he said as he held it up.

"I wanted you to be warm," she explained innocently. "'Course, you don't seem to be affected by the harsh winds of this place as I am, but…"

"No, I like it," he insisted. "Thank you. It's perfect. And we'll match."

She rolled her eyes and handed over the next box, almost cringing as he took it. "Now, this one," she prefaced, "might seem a little cheesy given you're a man. But the story that goes with it, hopefully, helps to remove the cheap factor. Open it first, and then I'll tell the tale."

Leif stared at the box, surmising its weight, then pulled at the ribbon. His excitement grew as he ripped through the pretty paper and opened the top. Inside was a small wooden chest complete with fake iron latches and a dome lid. At first glance, it looked like a pirate's treasure chest, but, once he took it out, he saw that it was a music box.

Immediately, he flipped it open, and a whimsical melody commenced, filling the room with a childlike air. He tried to appear thankful, though he wondered why she felt compelled to purchase it. Before he could offer his gratitude, she interceded.

"I know it's just a music box, but when I saw it at one of the gift shops in town, I had to get it. It reminded me of a story—a legend, actually. About a king and his chest."

Leif's thoughts flew straight to the chest he'd found. It was rather uncanny that her gift and his secret were based on a coffer, and he couldn't wait to tell her about it. "I like legends. My whole life's research is often based on debunking legends and exploring them."

"Then you're going to love this one," she said, shifting on the bed to sit with her legs tucked beneath her. After tugging and repositioning the sheet at her chest, she settled in and took a deep breath. "You'll have to excuse me if I mess this up. It was told to me so long ago, I hope I can remember it all." After a few passing breaths, she began her narration in fairy-tale fashion.

"There once was a king blessed with power, wealth, and dignity. He fell in love with a woman, and she loved him. For a time, they'd sneak out to meet each other. Sometimes to steal a kiss in the thickets of the garden. But always in brevity, for each was all too often called upon. Eventually, the king proposed an arrangement of marriage, but her father wouldn't allow it. He had other intentions of offering her to someone else—someone whose rising authority had threatened his holdings. By means of his daughter, he could secure favor and gain an ally instead of an enemy.

"One day, it was done. Her father married her to another, and not just any man, but coincidently, her own lover's sworn enemy. The king's heart broke in two, and he sank in deep despair. Rightly, he could've fought for her if he so chose, and won, for the size of his army was twice that of her husband's. But instead, he traveled as far away as he could from the woman who could no longer be his. He searched the ends of the world for the sweetest of oils, the rarest of silk, and the most beautiful of jewels he'd ever laid eyes on, and gathered them all in a wooden chest for his distant unattainable love. Unfortunately, his journey brought him many trials. It took him ten long years to return, but it was too late. His love had died.

"Now some say it was pneumonia, while others say 'twas a broken heart. Nonetheless, she died alone. You see, her husband had a reputation for making enemies everywhere he went, and he was constantly away fighting in battle. While he was frequently gone, she'd sneak out, waiting for her lover king to come back for her, but he never showed. It took all of nine years for her to assume that he'd found the arms of another before she finally gave up.

"After hearing the news of his love's death, the king couldn't keep the chest any longer. He'd traveled and searched for so long to give it to her that keeping it for himself destroyed the true meaning behind it. As he agonized in his own grief, he felt compelled to give the chest of valuables to her husband and end the feud between them, once and for all.

"The husband refused to accept the gift from the king, thinking it was a trick. He was unaware of the extensive value of the items within, and cast it aside. Still suspicious of the king's intentions, he stabbed him and left him for dead.

"In grave desperation, the king retreated south to a group of merchants who were preparing to set sail. He told his story on his deathbed. His exact words were that 'this chest must be given to the one who holds your heart.' And you, Leif Dæganssen, from the day I laid eyes on you, had my heart."

Leif sat motionless and stunned. He'd heard that tale before and could almost quote its ending verbatim, but he had no idea from whom or when.

A ginger touch upon his hand brought him out of his trance. "Leif?"

He swallowed, dying for a glass of water. "Yes?"

"Didn't you hear me?" Lorraine prompted. "I said from the day I laid eyes on you, you had my heart."

Leif undoubtedly heard her, but it wasn't her final words that rendered him speechless. It was the items in Lorraine's legendary tale that bore an incredible likeness to those in the chest he'd found. In all the time he'd spent researching through archives, historical documents, and even folklore, he never found anything relevant to his artifact until now. He had no proof that either were related, but he had a gut feeling he might have solved the mystery of his archeological find.

He grabbed her wrist and pulled her off the bed, leading her down the hall. "I have to show you something." She tripped many times on the sheet she held around her body, but kept up with him anyway. He stopped at his bedroom with his hand on the doorknob and looked at her. "What I'm about to show you is something very special to me and must remain between us. Only my brother knows about this. Can I trust you?"

Lorraine took hold of his free hand and squeezed. "Of course you can."

He turned the knob and burst through his bedroom door, hauling her inside just short of his bed. In the far corner, plastic covered the floor. On top of that were assorted brushes, a ruler, various picks, a trowel, camera, and a pad of paper with lots of scribbled notations. Beside his tools lay the remnants of the items Lorraine had mentioned in the king's chest, in neat rows and carefully labeled, and the tarnished and weathered chest itself.

Lorraine's heart stopped. She could hardly believe her own eyes. The very chest from her past that Dægan had given her as a wedding gift was staring her in the face.

"Where did you find this?" Lorraine asked, her voice shaking.

"Alongside my porch, just beneath my house."

She peeled her eyes from the coffer and gawked at Leif. So many questions bounced around in her head, yet she stood dumbfounded.

Leif seemed to understand her struggle and touched her shoulder. "Do you know what this is?" His own escalating excitement cut her answer short. "I think this might be the chest from your story." He directed her closer, and together they knelt beside the rare antiquities on Leif's floor. "Look," he demanded, pointing as he spoke. "The jewels, the jars of precious oils, the bolts of silks…they're all here, or what's left of them. I realize they don't look as impressive now as they probably did back then, but surely you can see past the grime and dust. As old as they are, they're remarkably well preserved."

As Lorraine listened to him praising the condition of the contents, she realized he was only in awe as an archeologist. Not as a man who'd recognized something extraordinary from his past. She felt nauseated and dizzy. Hot tears welled in her eyes, and the knot in her throat swelled to an unmerciful lump.

"I'm short of words as well," Leif said, misreading her outward emotions. "And to think I owe it all to you. I just wish I knew where I'd heard that story. I don't know... Maybe I read it somewhere, or heard one of the locals talking about it in the pub."

Leif's oblivious blabber crushed her spirit. She hung her head and covered her face with her hands. "I can't believe this."

Gingerly, he pulled her hands away and lifted her chin. "I'm so sorry, Raine," he said. "I'm such an insensitive jerk. You just gave me something from the heart, and I dismissed it coldly. I didn't mean to—"

"It's not that," she said. "I don't care about the stupid music box."

"What is it then?"

"You don't recognize the chest, do you?"

"But I do. Because of you, I believe I've uncovered an alliance endowment between an Irish chieftain and a Scandinavian merchant from the Dark Ages. Obviously, this is going to take more research, but I've already traced my ancestors to this very island. I have high hopes that someone from my lineage settled here and had knowledge of this chest."

Hearing Leif speak of it with such disconnection left her feeling dejected and disheartened. The roller coaster ride of emotions she'd endured in the last few minutes was more than she could stand. By all rights, he should've remembered the chest, and she couldn't understand why he hadn't.

"Are you crying?" he asked, brushing his thumb across her cheek. "Raine, please. Tell me what's wrong. I don't understand why you're upset."

"Because you don't remember anything," she whimpered, her voice choking behind the knot in her throat. "You don't remember who you are, who you used to be, what *we* used to be to each other."

Confusion filled his eyes. "I want to understand, but I'm having a difficult time following you. What do you mean, who we used to be?"

This was the moment she feared. The moment when she'd be forced to explain, knowing he wasn't ready to accept the unfathomable truth. The moment that would test what little strength and courage she had left.

Drawing a deep breath, she squared her shoulders. "Leif," she began. "You're the merchant to whom the dying king gave the chest. You're the Scandinavian foreigner who then offered the chest to the Connacht king as a peace offering. The chest is a wedding gift you gave me in hopes that I might realize how much you loved me."

Leif stiffened and slowly removed his hands from her face. He looked at her as though she'd spoken to him in an unknown language. Knowing she had to explain herself quickly, she reached for his hands and squeezed. "Let's go in a different direction," she proposed. "Where did you say you dug up the chest?"

"Beneath my porch, just outside the perimeter of my house."

She looked behind her in the room, getting her

bearings. "If I drew a straight line from here to the outside, is that where you found it?"

"Yes."

The incredulous tone of his one-word reply cut her like a dull knife, slow and excruciating. She stood up, gripping the sheet out of modesty, and examined the direction of the outer walls and the width of the room. Drawing an imaginary line with her hands based on the location of the buried chest, she roughly paced out the length of Dægan's home. "I need you to imagine a longhouse, running perpendicular from the lay of your cottage. Since you're an archaeologist, I assume you're aware of their general dimensions and layout. And it wouldn't be hard to envision your bedroom as the private closet-enclosed bedchamber sitting off the main room where a central hearth would exist."

"Raine—"

"No, please, let me finish. I beg you, let me explain."

An aggravated sigh huffed from his thinned lips, taking another piece of her heart. She trudged on, using details she knew he'd understand. She could only hope her firsthand knowledge of the tenth century would demonstrate that she wasn't mentally disturbed.

"In the days of Harald Fairhair and Niall Glundubh, you and I fell in love during a time of great upheaval. I was a princess of Connacht, and you were a mighty warrior chieftain and merchant of Norway, two very different people who should never have found love in each other. But we did. To protect me, you brought me here to Inishmore and we married, securing an alliance between the Irish natives of the island and your Norse family. You needed this alliance so you weren't forced to uproot your family again. We lived here," she said, recalling the days she'd spent in Dægan's longhouse. "We were husband and wife...and we were so happy." In thinking of how short-lived their joy was, her smile faded. "We were together for only a little over a fortnight. Your heinous brother came to the isle and, in revenge, took me from you. His name was Domaldr. He thought he'd killed you and all of your men, and he burned our homes to the ground so he'd be free to barter with my father, the Connacht king, Cathal Mac Conor. But you came for me. You and your great army saved me and, in turn, spared my father the fight he would have been faced with to save his reign. Tragically, you'd sustained many great wounds and after sailing back to the isle, you died in my arms. I held you as you took your last breaths."

The room was so quiet. She wasn't sure if Leif was silent out of respect or shock. Gathering her bravado once again, she wiped the tears from her face and sniffed. A slight hint of rain suddenly infused her senses. At first, she wrote it off as a common smell, given she was in Ireland, but the more she inhaled, the more prominent it became. She couldn't ignore it anymore.

"Do you smell that?" she asked timidly.

Leif stood, his face unreadable. "Smell what?"

"Rain," she stated matter-of-factly. "I smell rain."

He berated her with cold scorn. "We're in Ireland."

His harsh statement would have normally cut her to the quick, but a blissful warmth enveloped her as she drew in another long breath of rain. "The book!" she exclaimed. "It's here!"

Frantically, she looked around her, drawing in deep gulps of air as she tried to sniff out the whereabouts of St. Ciarán's Gospels.

Leif scratched his forehead. "What are you doing?"

"The book of St. Ciarán's Gospels… I smell it." With one hand securing the sheet to her body, she ripped open his closet doors, and the aroma of rain overwhelmed her. "Here." She pointed to the floor. "It's got to be buried here, beneath your floor. And that would make sense, because this is about the location of our bedchamber, where you hid it once before."

"Raine—"

She dropped to her knees, running her fingers along the baseboard, searching for a gap. "If you pull up this floor, I know you'll find it. And if you hold it in your hands, I know you'll remember. It was the book your father used to help your family survive a cruel winter when he was alive, and it's the same book you held fast to—"

"Raine," he said again, his voice rising.

"Help me," she pleaded. "It's here. You treasured this book almost as much as your father's sword, and if you'd just help me, I know we'll find it—"

Leif jerked her to her feet, his eyes as dark as midnight. "It's time for you to go."

She gathered the sheet that had nearly fallen away when he stood her upright, and gripped his arm in panic. "Please, don't do this. You have to believe me. You have to listen to what I'm telling you."

"I've heard enough," he said, dragging her back down the hall.

The icy grip of his hand around her elbow bit all the way to her bone. Leif had never acted this harshly toward her, and neither had Dægan. She had no idea what to do. Her heart bled for the chance to make him understand, but she didn't dare speak another word. It was obvious he needed some time to think and let it all sink in.

Stopping at the guest room, he glowered down his nose at her. "Get your things, and go."

Chapter Twenty-two

Lorraine gasped in long breaths as if her life depended on it. Leif was shoving her out of his life for good, and she couldn't do a thing to stop it. All that she'd worked so hard for was gone. All her hopes and dreams of reuniting with her long-lost love were vanishing. As he coldly ushered her into the guest room for her clothes, she made one more desperate plea.

"I know you're upset, Leif, but please think about how we connected so strongly with each other. There's a reason." She reached out to put her hand on his chest, hoping to depict being joined at the heart as he had done before, but he clasped her wrist and jerked it away.

"How dare you take the words from my heart and twist them to fit into an outlandish fabrication of lies. I cannot believe you'd be so low as to take my life's work and passion and turn it into a farce. I trusted you."

"And you still *can*," she insisted.

"Not anymore. You're not the woman I thought you were. All this time, I'd given you the benefit of the doubt, excusing your peculiar behavior and your strange outbursts for a head injury, when in fact you were just playing on my emotions, toying with my feelings. I'll admit, I was taken by you. I thought what we had was special. I might go so far as to say I was falling in love with you."

Lorraine felt her heart breaking and knew there was an impending "however" waiting to unfold.

"But I was a fool," he continued. "I was blinded by your beauty and deceived by your innocence."

More tears burned Lorraine's eyes. She felt as if she was stuck in the middle of a nightmare with no way to wake up. "I'm not lying to you. I would never lie to you. As God is my witness, what I've said is the honest truth. You are the reincarnated Dægan Ræliksen, my husband."

Devoid of emotion, Leif dismissed her heartfelt words. "And you're as crazy as a loon."

"Whoa..." Kristoff said, coming around the corner of the hallway.

After glancing between her and Leif, he seemed to realize that Leif's insult wasn't a playful joke. "I'll just come back."

"No," Leif retorted. "Lorraine was just leaving."

She held Kristoff's gaze for a few awkward moments, watching the brother battle against his intuition. "Seriously guys, I didn't know you were...and I should've knocked."

"It's not a problem," Leif snapped. "She's leaving." The blunt finality of his announcement was like a slap in the face, and the sting of his cruelty prickled under her skin.

"Better yet, Kristoff," Leif offered. "I'd appreciate it if you'd get her out of here."

Kristoff stammered. "Leif, don't you think that's a little harsh?"

Leif ignored his brother and glared at her. "You have but a few minutes to get your things, and go."

She had one last chance, a shot in the dark. "What about us? What about all we've shared?"

"The only thing we shared was an obsessive desire to encourage love when it never existed to begin with. One of us a little more fanatically than the other." He stormed into his bedroom and slammed the door.

She flinched at the blast of wood hitting wood, then turned to get dressed, her entire world crashing down around her.

****

Lorraine sat in Kristoff's carriage as the beautiful scenery of Ireland passed by. She couldn't appreciate the open meadows of wild roses and saxifrage. She couldn't feel the warm sun baking her in the Aran sweater she wore. She couldn't feel the bumps in the road jostling her about the bench. She was numb. Leif's final words and the slamming door were the only things she registered.

"Raine," Kristoff said as he climbed into the carriage with her. "What happened back there?"

Lorraine looked up, oblivious that the carriage had even come to a halt. He sat across from her, his eyes full of sympathy. He looked and sounded so much like Leif that the realization overwhelmed her to the point of tears. "I'm sorry, Kristoff. I can't." Gathering her things, she leapt from the carriage and ran to the safety of her cottage.

****

A knocked sounded on Leif's front door as he sat in his living room in a daze. Kristoff peeked in, then quietly closed the door behind him. "Want to tell me what hell is going on?"

Leif hardly acknowledged his brother. "Not really."

Kristoff crossed the room and sat beside him. "She's really upset."

Leif closed his eyes and flopped his head against the

back of the couch. Part of him didn't care that he'd broken her heart. He wanted to forget her and move on. The other part regretted what he'd said and how he'd treated her. He still yearned to run to her and take her in his arms, even though it went against everything he believed in to make up excuses for her neurotic behavior.

Confused and irritated, he also realized he had a confession to make to his brother. "You're not going to be happy with me."

Kristoff shrugged. "Won't be the first time."

"No, I mean it, and you'll have every right to be mad at me." He paused long enough to scrub his hands down his face. "I showed her the chest. I know I made you swear not to tell a soul, but I was weak, and I felt like I could tell Lorraine anything. I thought I could trust her."

Kristoff threw his arm above the couch and got comfortable. "So, what did she say that changed all that?"

Leif hesitated to explain. In his head, it all sounded ridiculous, and he knew his brother would think Lorraine was as nutty as a nine-bob note with her reincarnation story. It would kill him to hear his brother insult and make jokes about her. Instead, he stood up and headed for the kitchen. Coffee was what he needed. Strong coffee.

Kristoff followed him. "What did she say, Leif?"

"It doesn't matter. I let you down. I betrayed your trust when you gave me yours."

Kristoff slid into the closest chair at the table. "You're letting a good woman go because you'd rather beat yourself up for something you did to me? That doesn't make sense."

"It doesn't matter if it makes sense to you. Bottom line is I fell too fast for a woman and left my heart unguarded. Until this morning, I thought she was the one. End of story." With his hands braced on the counter, he watched the slow drip of coffee while his explanation to Kristoff cut deep.

End of story.

He didn't want their story to be over. It had only just begun. He recalled their lunch at Tí Joe Watty's, their private picnic at Dún Dúchathair watching the sun set, and their nightly walks along the beach. No matter where they went or what they did, it felt right to be with her. Especially when they kissed…

He called to mind the way he felt when their lips touched. If he could allow himself, just for a second, to believe they were lovers from a previous era, it would certainly explain the familiar sensations he felt each time he captured her lips, and the numerous déjà vu visions he had of her, reminiscent of a medieval era. But that was a big if.

Truth was, he didn't believe in that nonsense and refused to waste any more time on it. Somehow, someway, he had to free himself from the fierce knot she'd tied around his heart.

He swiped two coffee mugs from his cabinet. "You want coffee?"

Kristoff cleared his throat and leaned back in his chair. "If it tastes better than what you made last time, sure."

Leif poured their coffee and parked in the seat across from Kristoff, staring into his mug. "How do you detach yourself from a woman?"

Kristoff eyed him from the brim of his cup. "What?"

"How do you do it?" Leif asked, desperate for answers. "How can you be with all those women and not care about them? How do you walk away, especially after spending intimate moments with them?"

Kristoff crossed his arms and leaned back in his chair.

"I can forget because they mean nothing to me, and I mean nothing to them. But then again, I haven't found a woman I'd want to spend the rest of my life with. I'm sure my answer would be different then."

"So, you're really not mad at me for showing Raine the chest?"

"Not for that," Kristoff waved off. "I *am* mad at you for running her off when she was wrapped in nothing but a sheet. She was mighty easy on the eyes this morning."

"Is there not one ounce of couth in your body?"

"You say that as if you don't know me," Kristoff joked. He then took a long sip of his coffee, studying Leif. "So, I take it Lorraine's not coming to your party tonight?"

Shit. Leif completely forgot about the birthday party his brother concocted. "Honestly, I'm not really in the mood for it."

"You'll change your mind once you have a few pints in you."

"I'm afraid it's going to take more than a few pints."

Kristoff raised his mug. "Now that sounds like a man on a mission. As the man of the hour, you shouldn't have any problem forgetting her."

Clearly, Kristoff didn't understand the hold Lorraine O'Connor had on him. How could he when Leif barely understood it himself.

Chapter Twenty-three

Patrick had just finished showering from a long day of shoeing horses when he heard his phone ring from the next room. Wrapping a towel around his waist and assuming it was Beth calling to check on his status for their dinner date that evening, he padded into his bedroom to answer it. But when he picked up the cell, it wasn't Beth's image on the display.

"Hey, Raine. Nice to hear from you," he joked. But as soon as he heard her voice through the speaker, he knew she'd been crying. She rattled off something about ruining everything, a walk on the beach after dinner, and an Aran sweater. None of it made sense. "Hold on, slow down," he instructed kindly. "I can't understand you. You did what?"

"I ruined everything, Patrick. Leif wants nothing to do with me."

He sat on the edge of his bed, surprised that things had gone downhill so quickly. Last he'd heard, things were going great. "What do you mean he wants nothing to do with you?"

He listened intently to her whole story and tried to keep up.

"…and he told me to get my things and go."

Lorraine's last words jarred him. "Leif said this?" He found it hard to believe.

"Yes," Lorraine cried in exasperation. "He said the only thing he and I shared was an obsessive desire to encourage love when it never existed to begin with. Oh Patrick, what do I do? I've lost him. I've lost my only chance of being with him. I think I'm going to be sick. I need to come home."

Hearing the sheer panic in her voice and the heavy sobs of despair, he stood and paced the room. "Where are you now?"

"I'm in my room at the Man of Aran Cottage, but I'm coming home. I'm going to get online and book the next flight out of here."

"Raine, don't be rash. You still have more than a week left in Ireland. A lot can happen in the next few days. Maybe he needs some space. What you told him is a lot for a man to process. Give him time. Don't rush him."

"What if he never sees things the way I do?"

Patrick had no idea what to tell her. He sympathized with Leif and how he took the news. Finding out he might be the reincarnated soul of a Viking warrior who's married to a medieval princess was not something any man could digest easily. "We'll cross that bridge when we get there. Why did you tell him in the first place? I thought you were going to let nature take its course."

"I was, but this morning, he showed me something he'd dug up near his house. It was the chest he'd given me in the tenth century, the one you and I had talked about. He found it beneath the perimeter of his porch. I got excited because he was, and then next thing I knew, I was telling him everything."

His cell vibrated in his hand, notifying him of an incoming call. He glanced at the screen, and when he saw Beth's smiling face, his gut twisted. He stared at the display, uncertain if he should put Lorraine on hold and answer it, or ignore the call from his girlfriend with the intent to call her back.

Then he thought of how mad Beth would be if she knew he'd ignored her call for Lorraine's. Or the fact that he was seriously thinking of canceling their weekend plans to jet off to Ireland to help Lorraine. His chest tightened with guilt.

"Patrick?" he heard Lorraine call. "Are you still here?"

He clenched his fist, full of indecision, then swiped Beth's call away. "Yeah, I'm here."

"Oh, good. I thought we'd gotten disconnected." She blew her nose, then came back with, "Wait. Aren't you supposed to be with Beth tonight?"

He recoiled and tried to act as though it wasn't a big deal. "I am...but it's okay."

"No, it's not," she exclaimed. "You have to get off this phone with me and make that dinner you promised her."

"Trust me, I think the damage is already done."

"What do you mean?"

He sighed. "That was her, trying to call in, and I didn't answer."

"So, call her back."

"And tell her what? That your call was more important than hers? Truthfully, it is. But she won't understand that, and I can't lie to her. It's water under the bridge."

"Oh my gosh," she sobbed. "I've ruined two people's lives."

"It's not your fault, Raine," he consoled, already pulling up airline flights on his office computer. Knowing Beth wouldn't give him another second chance, or that he'd likely never see her again, he booked the first flight out of CVG and started packing a carry-on bag. "Stay where you are. I'm coming to you. I should be at your door by tomorrow afternoon."

Chapter Twenty-four

Leif put on his happy face as he entered Tí Joe Watty's with his brother, smiling gratefully at each happy birthday wish thrown his way. Many shook his hand or patted him on the back, while others made jests about his climbing age. Knowing it was all in good fun, he forced a laugh or two and headed straight for the bar.

Kristoff flagged down the bartender with two fingers, denoting the number of pints he wanted. Leaning on the bar, he looked around the crowded room and waved to a few smiling faces he'd recognized. "Did you see the woman standing next to Flanagan as we came in?"

Leif caught the pint glass that the bartender slid his way and took a large drink, downing half of it. He knew the redhead Kristoff mentioned was the woman his brother had a torrid one-night affair with a few months back. He also knew she'd run back to Flanagan, sparking another fire of competition between the two. "Of course I saw her."

"Did you see the look she gave me?"

"It was a congenial smile, nothing more. You'd do well to stay away from her."

Kristoff chuckled to himself as though Leif's warning barely registered. "Funny how Flanagan chose this night to bring her out, knowing I'd be here. He's goading me."

"Exactly. So, don't give him the satisfaction." In spite of Leif's advice, his brother glanced over his shoulder, offering a wink in the redhead's direction. "I mean it,

Kristoff. If you instigate anything tonight, you're on your own." Downing his Guinness, Leif felt another hard slap at his back and saw Dr. O'Donnell and his wife.

"There's the birthday boyo!"

"Dr. O'Donnell." Leif nodded in reply. "How are you this evening?"

"Well enough," he replied. "And how's Ms. O'Connor?"

"She's fine. Thanks." He'd endured the worst day without her, and unfortunately, he knew this wouldn't be last time someone asked.

"Where is she?" Dr. O'Donnell asked. "I figured the lass would be with you to celebrate this grand occasion."

Kristoff jumped in and saved him. "She couldn't make it tonight. Previous engagement. But we'll let her know you asked about her. Can I buy you and Mrs. O'Donnell a drink?"

"Nah, we're just heading out." Taking his wife by the hand, he nodded toward the brothers. "But thanks for the offer."

Leif watched the couple weave through the crowd, drifting into more thoughts of Lorraine. He wondered what she was doing, if she was spending her holiday in tears, or if she'd left posthaste. As much as he wanted to forget her and all the things she'd said, he couldn't. He'd fallen hard for her, and so quickly that he hadn't time to recover from the hole she'd left in his heart.

Kristoff waved a hand in front of his face. "You still in there?"

He shook away his morose thoughts and grabbed the other pint at the bar. "Yeah. Just thinking."

"That's your problem. You think too much. Come

on," Kristoff encouraged with a jerk of his head. "Let's go find a table."

Wishing he were anywhere but here, he followed Kristoff toward a table near the stage. He saw a few familiar faces and forced himself to appear excited, as it'd be rude otherwise. If his brother hadn't gone to so much trouble inviting friends from all across the planet, he wouldn't have come in the first place.

He spotted Mícheál in his kilt first, then his wife Catharina talking to Willie. Shaking hands with the guys, he accepted their over-the-hill jokes with a smile and a designated a few age jokes of his own for them. It had been a long time since he'd seen the two witty Irishmen, and he tried his best to live a little. Then Catharina walked up and cupped his face, greeting him with a compliment and a warm smile. "Look at you, you handsome devil. Happy birthday."

Leif wrapped his arms around her and reciprocated the welcome. "Thank you, Catharina. And you're as ravishing as ever."

"Watch it, Leif," Mícheál advised with a wink. "It may well be ye birthday but I'm not averse to blackening yer eye, if ye be needin' it."

"Don't listen to Mick." Catharina waved her hand dismissively. "He couldn't blacken a Cajun dish with a handful of cayenne peppers. You can flatter me anytime you want."

Kristoff elbowed Willie. "Looks like the kilted hasher brought his feelings with him. Couldn't you've left those at the door, Mick, along with those white balusters you call legs?"

Laughter erupted, and it was like old times as jests and jibes flew off at every turn. Despite Leif's heart longing for

Lorraine, he was beginning to enjoy himself.

Gazing at the other end of the table, he took notice of Karen, Willie's wife, sitting quietly as the men continued to berate each other. He took a seat beside her and smiled. "Thanks for coming, Karen. It's a lovely surprise to see you and Willie again."

"It's nice to see you too," Karen replied, holding up her bottle of Smithwick's. "Happy birthday."

"Thank you."

"So, where's this woman of yours? Kristoff said we'd meet her tonight."

Leif cleared his throat and leaned back in his chair. "I'm afraid my brother jumped the gun again. She won't be here."

"Ah, that's too bad. I was looking forward to adding another female to our group of friends." She pointed toward Kristoff, Willie, and Mícheál, who were clinking their mugs and chugging pints. "We've enough testosterone as it is."

Before Leif could add his thoughts on the matter, a hardy male voice came over the loud speaker. "Tonight, we're all here to celebrate the birthday of Leif Dæganssen."

Leif looked over his shoulder to see his good friend and musician John Tracey at the microphone with a Maton guitar strapped to his body and a pint of Guinness in his hand. He smiled as a collective silence filtered through the crowd and prepared himself for the announcement to follow.

"On behalf of Fretwear, our little two-man band, and all the good people of Tí Joe Watty's, it gives me great pleasure to dedicate the first song to the man of the hour. It's a song Kevy and I wrote together called 'Women,

Whiskey, and Beers,' and from the look of this place, there's plenty of that afoot here. *Breithlá sona duit, a Leif a fhir!'*

A strong salute of cheers and toasts rose up all around him, and John strummed the first few bars of the song. Between the picking talents of John's fingers and Kevin's soulful voice, the bluesy tunes that lit up the frets of John's Tommy Emmanuel-autographed flat box catered specifically to Leif's mood. He didn't want to be here. He wanted to be in Lorraine's arms.

Song after song, he sat at the table, mindlessly listening to the conversations that bounced back and forth between his friends. As he nodded from time to time and pretended to hang on their every word, he imagined all the things Lorraine had said to support her reincarnation story. There was the fact that she'd quoted names of prominent men in history, who he knew played a part in his ancestors' world. And she gave details so explicit, only a fellow archaeologist or historian would know.

"In the days of Harald Fairhair and Niall Glundubh, you and I fell in love during a time of great upheaval."

Akin to what she'd described and from what he'd gathered in all his research over the years, his ancestors had moved from Hladir to the Aran Islands. Though for reasons he'd yet to uncover, Lorraine had claimed they'd relocated because they were forced to uproot, and then stayed in Ireland because of an alliance. What's more, she delineated the parameters of a Scandinavian longhouse complete with the usual furnishings of a central hearth, perimeter bench seating, and an enclosed bed-closet for the master of the house and his wife. A bartender from Kentucky wouldn't normally know of such things unless…

Unless she lived through it.

It was hard to believe, yet on the flip side, it was only thing that made sense.

If she were reincarnated, she'd know about Irish kings, marriage arrangements, and alliances. If she once lived in the tenth century, she'd be able to describe the look and feel of a Scandinavian longhouse without blinking an eye.

Leif's head pounded as his thoughts raced through fact and fiction. He wanted more than anything to trust what she'd said was true, but if he took her story as gospel, then he'd also have to believe that he too had lived a previous life, married to her.

He looked around at the change of a song and saw his friends dancing in pairs, swaying to the quiet rhythm of John's moving instrumental. To his astonishment, he also noticed his brother embracing a certain redhead on the dance floor.

Shit.

As always, Kristoff did whatever he wanted, and as expected, Flanagan came storming through the pub in his brother's direction.

Chapter Twenty-five

Noting the fury on the Flanagan's face, Leif lunged from his seat and blocked the Irishman from his unaware brother. Flanagan halted, peering over Leif's shoulder in rage.

"Keep your womanizing brother away from my sister!"

Leif couldn't believe his ears. Surely, he heard wrong. "Your sister?" he asked. All this time, Kristoff had assumed the woman was Flanagan's girlfriend because of how protective and angry Flanagan was after their one-night affair. If Kristoff found out she was only a sibling, there'd be no stopping him.

"Yes, my sister," Flanagan bit out. "If he thinks he's going to weasel his sorry arse into Maggie's bed again, he's got another thing coming."

Leif grabbed Flanagan by the arm and pulled him back. "It doesn't have to go down like this, Flanagan."

"Take your hands off me, Dæganssen."

"I understand how you feel when it comes to my brother's reputation, but he's only dancing with Maggie. There's no harm in that. When the song is over, I'll kindly split them up, and you can be on your way."

"I don't need your assistance," Flanagan sneered, jerking his arm free.

"Then at least take my advice," Leif said sternly. "Don't let Kristoff know she's your sister."

Barreling past Leif, Flanagan stomped through the

crowd and yanked the woman from Kristoff's arms. The noise of the room kept Leif from hearing the words they'd exchanged, but to his relief, Kristoff stood there as Flanagan led the woman out the door.

After a few awkward glances from the people who witnessed the scene, Kristoff made a beeline for the bar. By the time Leif caught up to him, he'd already ordered a double shot of Jameson.

Leif leaned against the bar, knowing the battle that raged in his brother's head. "Do you really think you need that right now?" he asked, gesturing toward the caramel-colored fluid brimming in the glass.

Kristoff shot the alcohol without so much as looking at Leif. Slamming the empty glass on the bar, he ordered another. "Did you do this?"

"Do what?"

"I saw you talking to Flanagan. Did you—"

"No. I didn't. But I did stop him from knocking your teeth out."

Kristoff laughed cynically. "I'd like to see Flanagan try. And I'd like *you* to stay out of my business."

"You're my brother. You are my business."

This time, a scoff erupted from Kristoff's lips before he tossed back the second shot. "What happened to the 'if you instigate anything tonight, you're on your own' mentality?"

"Are you trying to pick a fight with me now?"

Kristoff slid the empty glass away and turned to glare at Leif. "No, I'm not picking a fight with you. I'm—"

"Everything all right?" Willie asked as he and the others approached the bar.

Leif smiled and patted his brother's back.

"Everything's fine. Kristoff just needs to sleep this off."

"Looks like someone else forgot to leave their feelings at the door," Mícheál jibed.

"Something like that," Leif concluded as he noticed Kristoff's eyes glazing over. "I want to thank you all for coming on such short notice. It was great to see you again. Do you need a lift to where you're staying for the night?"

Willie wrapped his arm around Karen. "I suspect we're going to stay for a few more songs, and then we'll catch a cab. Thanks for the offer, though."

Leif hugged his friends good-bye, and when he got to Karen, she whispered, "I can tell you missed your lady friend tonight. Don't let her get away, you hear?"

He nodded once and grabbed Kristoff by the shirt, dragging him toward the door. "Let's go. You're staying at my place tonight."

"Fine."

Leif held the door for his dispirited brother. As soon as they stepped outside, a shrill scream broke through the brisk night air. The brothers exchanged glances, then took off toward the cry for help, past the beer garden and around the darkened corner of the pub. In the dimly lit area beside the trees, they saw two men scuffling with a woman pinned against the wall.

"Maggie!" Kristoff exclaimed, darting to her rescue and slugging the first man he got a hold of.

Leif followed without hesitation and came in swinging at the other. A fight broke out between the four men, with punches flying and garbage cans overturning. Leif eventually tackled one to the ground, and before he could beat the guy to a pulp, Maggie screamed Kristoff's name. Distracted, Leif caught a fist across his jaw, and the man squirmed from underneath him, escaping into the night. He shook it off and scanned the shadows just in time to see his brother jerk the remaining mugger up by his shirt and slam him against the wall.

"Big man, aren't you, attacking a woman like that," Kristoff spat scathingly. He punctuated it with a solid punch to the assailant's gut, but immediately doubled over and fell to his knees.

Panic and fear shot through Leif like splintered ice. He could only see that his brother collapsed on the ground, but he didn't know why. As he scrambled to his feet and ran to Kristoff, the scene before him altered like a swiftly changing dream. He no longer ran on a cobblestone-paved alley beside the pub. Instead, he was sliding to his knees inside a dirt-packed barn.

"Sh...brother. You're going to be fine." I lied, and Mara knew it. The large amount of blood pouring from Eirik's wound in such a quick amount of time meant a vessel had been direly severed. Nothing could save him, no matter what we tried.

I pushed my palm firmly against the wound and held steady pressure, but the blood oozed between my fingers and seeped around my hand. "Eirik...stay with me. Look at me, brother. Look at me."

Eirik moaned in pain, then coughed. I pushed my palm harder against the gaping wound. "No, Eirik! No!" I leaned closer to my brother's face and encouraged him to speak. "That's it, Eirik. Tell me. Tell me who did this." As I cradled my brother, he reached for my forearm, then his hand dropped lifelessly to the ground.

"No, Eirik! No!" Leif called out. He trembled as he stared at his injured brother lying on the ground in Maggie's arms.

Maggie and Kristoff looked at him as if he had three

heads. "Who's Eirik?"

Still disoriented between what he'd envisioned and what really happened, Leif was slow to realize that his brother was alive and well. "Are you sure you're all right?"

"I'm fine," Kristoff said, cradling his groin. "I just took a shot to the bollocks." He guardedly climbed to a standing position and pulled Maggie into his embrace. He cupped her face, wiping her tears with his thumb. "What about you? Did they hurt you?"

"No," she cried, sinking into his arms again. "I'm fine now, thanks to you."

"What the devil happened here?" Flanagan's voice exploded from behind them, and he reached for Maggie, ripping her from Kristoff's arms. When he saw her shirt had been torn open, his eyes lit up in flames. "I knew you were a womanizing bastard, but I didn't think you would were capable of *this*."

Leif hustled to his feet and charged Flanagan. "You've got this all wrong, Flanagan."

"Then how do you explain my sister in tears and the condition of her blouse?"

"Why don't you ask the two lowlifes that took off toward the pier? If it wasn't for Kristoff, she'd have suffered more than that."

Flanagan stilled as Leif's words settled in his head. "Is this true, Maggie?"

As if suddenly self-conscious, she crisscrossed her arms over her chest and held her shirt closed. Kristoff unbuttoned his shirt and threw it around her shoulders, holding her against his body. She smiled halfheartedly, still shaking. "Yes, it's true. Kristoff came to my rescue. He and Leif."

Flanagan let out a hiss and paced. Leif knew he was

finding it hard to accept that Kristoff was not the scoundrel he thought him to be. After a few paces, Flanagan approached Maggie. "I'm sorry I wasn't there to protect you. I shouldn't have left you alone."

"Yeah, why did you?" Kristoff questioned.

Flanagan glared at him. "I was only gone for a moment. I left her at the door to pull up the carriage." Silence followed, and the tension remained until Flanagan finally let down his pride. He stuck out his hand and looked Kristoff in the eye. "Thank you."

Kristoff hesitated, but eventually shook hands with the Irishman. "She's cold. Get her home safe."

Flanagan wrapped his arm around Maggie and ushered her away, leaving Kristoff with a proud smile. Leif joined his brother as they watched the two walk around the corner and disappear into the night.

"Did you hear that?" Kristoff asked. "Maggie's his sister."

Leif shook his head. "I was hoping you didn't catch that."

Kristoff let out a laugh, then groaned and cradled his groin. "That's not the only thing I caught." When Leif laughed, he said, "I swear they're in my throat. Look," he said, opening his mouth. "Can you see them?"

Whether in fun or not, Leif refused to look for his brother's testicles and began the long walk home. The flow of adrenaline tapered off and, in due course, so did the deadening effect of the alcohol they'd consumed. Leif rubbed his jaw while Kristoff hunched over and limped all the way down the road. The two men nursed their aching bodies in silence until Kristoff piped up with an interesting question.

"Who's Eirik?"

Chapter Twenty-six

Leif asked himself that very question. Who *was* Eirik, and why had he appeared at such a poignant moment? The entire journey home, he couldn't answer Kristoff's question, nor could he solve the mystery for himself. The only two things he knew for sure was that he'd called Eirik his brother, and Lorraine was there beside him. But strangely, the name Mara, instead of Raine, registered in his head at the time of the vision.

In a deep stupor, he entered his cottage and said good night to his brother, who collapsed on his couch. He walked like a zombie down the hall and stopped at the door of his guest room. When he peered in, his heart ached at seeing the empty bed.

The room was just as Lorraine had left it that morning. The blankets and sheets were disheveled on the mattress, bringing to mind the nights he'd spent making love to her and waking up with her body snuggled against his. Without her, there was an emptiness inside him, and he could barely deal with the notion of sleeping alone.

He climbed across the bed and buried his head in the pillow, smelling the scent she'd left behind. Spiced cinnamon and warm cypress. He savored it, clutching the fragrant cushion at his chest. He needed her, now more than ever. He felt lost and alone, wandering the depths of uncertainty with no knowledge of what to look for. He had so many unanswered questions, and most of them could probably be resolved through Lorraine, if he took the time to listen.

He recalled the look in her eyes when he'd told her to leave. He'd thrown away every precious moment they'd shared with just a few words, and for what? Pride? He wanted to believe everything she'd said about who he was and the reason he'd felt a deep connection with her. If for no other reason than because she claimed it the God's honest truth.

Frustrated with himself and his indecision, he kicked his legs out and sprawled across the mattress. Something heavy hit the floor, and he sat up, looking over the foot of the bed. There, in a pile of boxes, crumpled tissue paper, and a forgotten Aran sweater, he saw the carved wooden music box Lorraine had given him.

His heart leapt as he retrieved the gift from the floor. Lying back upon the bed, he wound it up and popped open the lid. The clear tinkling of the melody soothed the aggravation from his mind and brought a smile to his face. He thought of the legendary story she'd told him about the chest and the words she said to him thereafter: *"...and you, Leif Dæganssen, from the day I laid eyes on you, had my heart."*

Serenaded by the quiet, simple song, he lay there thinking of Lorraine's laughter and the happiness she'd provided him. As his eyes fluttered heavily, he made a final decision. First thing in the morning, he'd go to her.

****

With the music box in hand, Leif raced bareback up the paved road on Thor. The sound of the horse's hooves pounded out a rhythm that matched the pace of his beating heart. He was excited to see Lorraine and determined to forget all that he knew to be real and fathomable. For her, he'd open his mind to the possibility of reincarnation.

Their souls reborn were all he had to go on at the moment. Nothing else explained the unusual emotions and familiar sensations he had when he was with her. Against his better judgment, he started to believe that perhaps the extraordinary visions he'd seen were past memories resurfacing. But that meant he'd have to embrace a whole new set of doctrines and beliefs for which there were no scientific grounds. If it meant he'd somehow bridge the gap between him and Lorraine, then he was willing to put all academic theories aside.

As he reached the Man of Aran Cottages, he halted his horse and took in the picturesque view. The long, single-story buildings sat side by side of each other, the pitch of their roofs creating an M-shaped appearance. The outside structure was made of stone, painted bright white with stained wood panes framing the windows. A narrow walkway bordered by a knee-high rock barrier ran the length of the quaint cottages, while roses of various vibrant colors clung to its walls. Though improvements on the thatched cottages had been made over time, the Old World charm remained.

Dismounting, he threw the reins over his horse's back and walked to the farthest cottage, assuming Lorraine would prefer the view of the Atlantic from her window. His legs felt heavy and sluggish, as if he'd made the jaunt from his house to here himself. His mind raced, and he didn't know what he'd say once she opened the door. His nerves jittered as he realized he was clueless how to greet her. The last time he'd seen her, he'd been rude, and there was a good possibility she'd slam the door in his face. Worse yet, she might have already packed her things and split town.

The idea of Lorraine on a plane bound for Kentucky left him with a dreadful feeling. He'd kick himself if he'd missed his chance to repair the hurt he'd caused her. He couldn't live with himself if he knew he'd deserted her without a word of apology or explanation.

Stopping at the first door he came to, he drew in a long breath and knocked. Despite the cool, damp breeze whistling in his ears, he heard voices—Lorraine's voice, he thought, and someone else he didn't recognize. Maybe he didn't have the right room. He leaned forward to listen and innocently eavesdropped on those inside.

The door flew open, and Leif straightened, shocked at seeing a dark-haired fellow of middle age standing before him. He noticed a twinge of irritation registering on the man's face, and Leif figured he was likely a honeymooning husband annoyed by the interruption.

"I'm sorry," Leif apologized. "I have the wrong room."

"I wish that were true, Leif," the man retorted, stepping aside.

From inside the cottage, Lorraine approached the door with a look of confusion. "You two know each other?" she asked.

Leif studied the man but couldn't place why he looked familiar.

"Yes, we know each other," the man said. "I shod his horse a few years ago. That Friesian beauty, to be exact."

Realization struck Leif. "Patrick..." he said, coming up short on his last name. "I'm sorry I can't recall—"

"O'Rorke," Patrick answered for him.

"Right," Leif said, nodding. As the awkwardness mounted, he directed his attention back to Lorraine, but words failed him. He'd forgotten why he'd come. His mind was whirling with why the farrier was rooming with her, and then it hit him. He remembered the conversation he'd had with Lorraine on the beach the night before. Putting two and two together, he derived that Lorraine went running back to the man she'd always counted on, the man she claimed was just a friend. He wasn't stupid. He knew exactly what was going on between them, especially once he glanced down and saw the way Patrick held her hand.

Jealousy reared inside him. When he clenched his fists, he felt the music box in his hand and remembered his purpose for being there. But it didn't matter anymore. The words she'd spoken to him when she'd given the gift no longer held meaning.

He took one last look at her and returned it. "I guess I'm not the only one who holds your heart."

"Leif, wait!"

He heard the sheer desperation in her plea, but he ignored it and stomped toward his horse. He didn't even give her a second look when he swung his leg up and mounted. He grabbed the reins and sped away, leaving his broken heart bleeding at her feet.

****

Patrick stared at Lorraine crying in a crumpled heap on the floor of the cottage. Every muscle in his body ached to hold her. He couldn't let himself give in to temptation, for he feared if he took her in his arms, he'd never let her go.

He squatted before her and kindly lifted her tearstained face. He tenderly wiped her cheeks with his thumbs and looked at her for a few quiet moments, knowing he was standing at a point of no return.

"Do you love him?" Patrick asked, his voice quaking. He hated the sound of it, and hoped she'd not think him weak. What he was about to do required more strength than he thought he possessed. "I said, do you love him? Answer me, Raine."

"With all my heart, I love him," she professed. "I can't live without him. He is my life. My reason for living. And he's gone." She glanced back at the empty winding road. "I've lost him again. He'll never come back."

Patrick ignored the pain in his heart and pulled her attention back to him. "Do you trust me?"

"W-what are you talking about?"

"It's a simple question, Raine. For the love of God, do you trust me?"

"Of course, I trust you."

"Then promise me you'll stay here while I talk with Leif." She stammered as if trying to understand his demand. "I'm going to fix this," he reassured her. "I'm going to make everything all right, but you have to promise you'll stay here. Understand?"

Lorraine nodded hopelessly. "What are you going to say to him?"

Patrick felt his spirits plummet. "I don't know yet. I'll figure it out."

"He'll never listen to you."

He wiped her tears, one by one, his thoughts only on making her smile again. "Never say never."

Chapter Twenty-seven

Leif removed Thor's headstall and threw it wildly across the barn. He needed to vent, to punch something. Patrick's face would fit the bill nicely, and for a second, the idea tempted him to race back up the road.

The image of Patrick holding Lorraine's hand ate at him like acid, burning and stinging all the way through. It was bad enough that she'd wasted no time replacing him, but to know it was with someone he'd once respected drove him crazy.

Patrick was a knowledgeable farrier who'd gone out of his way to shoe Thor after a sale. Though their encounter was brief, Leif could tell he was a genuinely good fellow. They'd made conversation during the hour it took to fit his horse with size four shoes, and he recalled Patrick charged him next to nothing for the job. Making his acquaintance was the only thing that saved Patrick. Leif would rather not have known him at all so he'd feel no remorse after breaking his nose.

Kicking at a stall door as he passed by, he led his horse out of the barn and into the back lot. Freyja met them at the entrance of the pasture, nickering as she always did, while Leif took out his anger on the stone gate. He ripped a gap in the rock fence with a furious swipe of his arm, and took great pleasure in slamming a few heavy stones to the ground. Thor and Freyja, with their gentle demeanors, stared at him with ears alert until his temper subsided.

Leif planted his hands on his hips and stared into the distant horizon, the picture of Lorraine with Patrick still dancing in his head. If not for Thor nudging him, he would've stood there for hours, stewing over how foolish he felt.

He turned and stroked a gentle hand down Thor's muzzle, feeling the tension leave his body. He patted Thor's neck and buried his nose in the horse's mane, leaning on his horse for support. "I don't want to let her go," Leif muttered.

"Then don't."

Leif whirled around at the voice behind him and locked eyes with the last man he expected to see. "What the hell are you doing here?"

Patrick took a step forward and picked up one of the rocks from the ground. "We have to talk."

"I've nothing to say to you," Leif growled. "And I doubt you have anything I'd want to hear."

"Even if it pertained to Lorraine's happiness?"

He never dreamed Patrick would be so bold as to trespass on his land and flaunt his love for Lorraine in his face. "If she's happy with you, then I'm happy for her. You two have my blessing. Satisfied?"

"Hardly," Patrick muttered.

Leif ignored him and unfastened Thor's halter, hoping by the time he turned around Patrick would be gone. But the man had already begun gathering the scattered rocks and piling them back into place, killing him with kindness. He stormed forward and lifted Patrick to his feet by the collar of his shirt. "Get off my land. *Now!*"

Patrick smiled. "It's amazing how familiar this is."

Leif furrowed his brow and tightened his grip on Patrick's clothing. "How familiar what is?"

"You and I. In love with the same woman. Only last time, you didn't back down. You couldn't stand the thought of another man loving her. So, why are you giving up now? It's not like you."

Leif threw him backward, uncomfortable with Patrick's scrutiny. "I have no idea what you're talking about."

"You would if you weren't so stubborn."

Leif clenched his teeth until he thought they'd crack under the pressure. He balled his hands into tight fists, bristling at the insult.

"Why is it so hard for you to believe in the truth, Northman?" Patrick continued. "The clues are all around you. You even dug them up beneath your very house. Do we have to spell it out for you?" He stepped closer, boldly getting within arm's reach. "When you and I first met, and you told me what you did for a living, I thought to myself, this will be a piece of cake. Between Lorraine's dreams and your knowledge of historical events, all I had to do was get the two of you in the vicinity of each other and let history repeat itself, as it often does.

"It worked like a charm. Nature took its course, and everything was going according to plan, until you got scared."

Leif wasn't scared. He'd been ready to commit to her and blindly jump into a relationship based on nothing but a gut feeling. Loving her with all his heart and making her his wife were not the actions of a frightened man. It was the notion of *why* she loved *him* that had caused him to pull away.

Leif had tried to imagine himself as a reincarnated soul, but the idea was just too much to handle. If he'd lived a previous life as a Norse warrior and husband, then why didn't he remember?

He thought of what Patrick had said. "Lorraine dreamed about me?"

"For as long as I've known her," Patrick admitted. "And it was always the same dream, you kissing her. She knew the feel of your lips before she met you. Trust me, she was skeptical at first. But after you kissed her at Dún Dúchathair, all doubt vanished. Not even centuries of time could erase the feel of love's first kiss. Honestly, I'm a little surprised you didn't feel it."

Leif looked away. He *had* felt something but never understood what it was. Patrick noticed.

"You did feel something," he amended. "Admit it, you flashed back to a moment when you were with Mara."

The name caught Leif off guard, like a sobering douse of ice-cold water in the face. He'd only recently learned of the name himself and never spoke of it to anyone. Not even Lorraine. How would Patrick know the name of the woman he'd seen in his dream?

Patrick looked as if he were waiting for the other shoe to drop. When it didn't, he threw his hands up. "Why do you fight this? I figured you of all people would be thrilled to know your past. You were a man of great importance in your time. You were a wealthy warrior and chieftain from the fjords of Norway who fell in love with a Connacht princess and made the ultimate sacrifice to protect her. How can you not embrace this incredible revelation and realize you've been given another chance to be with the woman you died for? It's not as if this happens every day, Leif. Put your damn pride aside and seize this opportunity before it's too late!"

Leif stared at him. "Who are you?"

"I'm the reincarnated soul of the man who spared you

from the crimes of your evil brother, Domaldr. As your twin, he posed as you to steal your wife and wreak havoc on the Connacht king. I saved you so you could come for her. You brought an army twice the size of your brother's and left a field of dead bodies in your wake. But you still needed to breach the king's walls. You needed me in order to be reunited with your wife and secure a truce with her father. I know Lorraine's told you all this, but she failed to mention my name because she has no recollection of me. And I plan to keep it that way."

Leif advanced in Patrick's direction and stopped a few inches from his face. "Give me a name." He saw the muscles in Patrick's jaw clench as though he were reluctant to say.

"I'm Breandán Mac Liam," he finally said. "I'm the man you hated as much then as you do now because I loved her too. But no matter what happens after this, Lorraine must never know my identity. Swear you'll keep my secret."

"Why should I care?" Leif asked snidely.

"Because if she finds out, I fear you'll never have all her love as you should. She'll remember that I too loved and married her, after you were gone from this earth."

Leif wanted to laugh in spite of himself. "If you love her so much, then why are you so adamant that I take her from you? Why push the woman you once married into another man's arms?"

"For reasons I'd think you'd understand. Or at least Dægan would. Dægan would give anything to make her happy, because that's what true love is." Patrick turned away and gazed into the distance, as if he could see the memories from his past playing out among the nostalgic fields of Inishmore. "When I came to Mara seven years after your death, she was lost without you. She bore your son, Lochlann, and raised him to be proud of his Norse father. But the void you left behind was great. She was never the same again. Because of my love for her, I told her that if I could, I would gladly switch places with you, just so she could be happy again. I think she believed me. But even after she and I married, I could never make her as happy as when she was with you. Believe me, I tried. God, I tried."

Patrick faced him now, a sense of conviction burning in his eyes. "For whatever reason, I've been given that chance. To sacrifice my love for her so that I could give her the one thing that would make her truly happy. I know you love her. You wouldn't have come back for her if you didn't. So please, don't walk away. She needs you, and I know there's a part, deep down inside you, that needs her as well."

Leif closed his eyes. He could feel the earnestness of Patrick's words and was moved by his sincerity. But rousing an emotion was not the same as feeling it. His heart and mind were void of all that might or might not have happened from a previous life. He had no memory of a historical past and therefore couldn't connect. He turned his back on Patrick and began restoring the stone wall he'd torn down. "You have the wrong man."

"Has nothing I said meant anything to you?" Patrick's voice rose. "How can you be so aloof when the woman you love is dying up there? Tear by precious tear, her heart is breaking because you're too stubborn to take her in your arms and love her like you know you want to!"

Leif methodically picked up the rocks and placed them on top of one another, striving to keep his emotions in check. Try as he might, Patrick's words hit their mark on his heart. Inside, he was bruised and powerless, aching to be the haughty warrior Patrick claimed him to be, yearning to be the man Lorraine had dreamed about all her life. But without those memories, he was nothing more than a puppet on a string, performing a role for the sake of someone else's wishes.

Patrick lunged toward him and wrenched him to his feet. "Look me in the eye and tell me you don't love her."

Leif shoved his hands away, his blood boiling. "I don't have to tell you anything. Get off my land before I throw you off."

"What kind of man are you?" Patrick waited for an answer, then waved him off out of impatience. "You're nothing but a two-bit seducing philanderer."

It happened before Leif could stop it. He drove his fist hard into Patrick's face, knocking him off balance. Patrick quickly straightened himself and spat blood from his mouth.

"I didn't come here to fight with you, Leif. I came here for Lorraine. It's obvious you've built walls around your heart so thick that not even Dægan would have the might to break them down. You'll never know who you truly are until you find out for yourself. I can only hope it's not too late when you do."

"You threatening me, Irishman?"

"No," Patrick stated matter-of-factly. "I wouldn't dream of such a thing. But know this. In a few days, we'll be leaving Ireland for good. Once Lorraine and I get on that plane, you'll never see her again. I won't let her spend another lifetime pining for a man who doesn't exist. I'll slander your name to the ground if I have to, but when I'm finished, she won't remember you. All she'll remember is how you threw away her love like a piece of garbage."

"You do what you have to do."

Patrick touched his thumb to his swollen lip. "What Lorraine has told you is the honest truth. There's no denying who you are. But until you go in that house and dig up the evidence for yourself, you'll never know who you used to be. Rest assured, you'll realize it one day, and by then, it'll be too late. Don't be a fool and let the only woman you've ever loved slip through your grasp. Three days, Leif."

Chapter Twenty-eight

Seething with a degree of madness he'd never known before, Leif stormed up his porch steps with an ax in his grip. He burst through the front door and trudged through his house, a man on a mission. Once and for all, he was going to prove to everyone that he was not a Viking warrior reincarnated in an archaeologist's body.

As he turned the corner of the hall, Kristoff called after him and then noticed the shiny blade in his possession. "What are you doing with an ax?"

Leif continued his crusade down the hall and slammed the door in his brother's face. He ignored Kristoff jiggling the knob and talking to him through the wood, because he was too busy staring at the double doors of his closet.

The smell of rain surrounded him when he ripped them open. Just as Lorraine had claimed that night. Logic told him his thatched roof had begun to leak again, but he couldn't ignore his main objective.

"I thought you and I could finish the longship today," he heard Kristoff say. He paused, and asked again, "Seriously, Leif, what are you doing with the ax?"

His brother's persistence rubbed his last nerve, and he pounded on the wall. "Get out!"

Leif didn't care that his brother cursed him to hell, or that he slammed his front door as he left. The only thing on his mind was getting below the planks of his wood floor. Leaning the ax against the wall, he grabbed the closet door and jerked it off its track. He did the same to the other and shoved his hanging clothes aside, clearing an open path for the ax.

Gauging where he'd chop first, he noted the tongue and groove of the planks, then took hold of the ax and brought it down between the joint, splitting the relatively old floor. Having no trouble breaking through with the first swing, he lined up the blade on another spot and began to chop a splintered hole. He destroyed the floor plank by plank, until the opening was large enough for his shoulders to pass through.

Dropping to his knees, he peered inside. The aroma of a daylong deluge met him in the face like a blunt force. He had no clue as to why he smelled rain from beneath his house, but he couldn't rightly argue with his nose. He smelled it.

He lowered his head farther into the hole, but couldn't see a thing. He got to his feet, then ran to the kitchen and snatched a flashlight from the drawer. He ran back to his bedroom and returned to the hole, then crammed his body inside. He hung upside down from his waist and found nothing but a dirt-packed crawl space with vents and pipes running the lengths of the joists.

Disappointment crushed him, and he realized then how much he'd wanted to find proof that he was, in fact, Dægan Ræliksen. At this point, he would've appreciated a mere glass bead or an old wooden spool from a weaving loom, just to verify that his house sat atop some sort of historical settlement. A Scandinavian one would be better, but no such luck. He found nothing until he started to heave himself out of the hole and a flicker of something shiny glinted in the beam of the flashlight.

He held his breath and directed the light back over the

area. A tiny sliver of tarnished metal gleamed like a diamond. When he stretched to grab it, his shirt snagged on the broken fragments of the floor and kept him from reaching it. He resurfaced from the hole and drove his boot heel against the remaining planks, widening the opening.

As his adrenaline surged, he grabbed a few of his archaeology tools that sat beside the chest on the bedroom floor and dove all the way in. He crawled on his stomach across the dirt, and with expert hands, though trembling with excitement, he painstakingly brushed away the soil a little at a time. Bit by bit, the grandness of the object emerged. He still had no idea what he'd found, but eventually, a combination of gold and silver materialized on what looked like the hilt of a dagger.

The minutes of the afternoon turned into hours as he worked to unearth the small artifact. By late evening, he was able to pluck the object from its delicate grave of dry dirt and ascend from the crude site of his do-it-yourself dig.

He placed the item on the plastic sheeting on his floor and realized the sun had already set. Darkness filled the room, save for the fading glow of his dying flashlight. He jumped to his feet and flipped the light switch, then returned to get a good look at the piece he'd found.

As he suspected, it was a knife, but until he could clean it thoroughly, he couldn't discern its value. Using only a soft-bristled toothbrush and water, he cleaned the hilt of the dagger, removing the grime that had worked its way into every crevice of the elaborately decorated weapon.

After hours of tedious work, he held the dagger in his palm. He stared in awe at the craftsmanship of the handle, his tired mind drifting into oblivion...

"Which would you prefer to do?" I asked, extending both the ax and dagger for her choosing. "Fillet the fish, or cut the wood for kindling?"

She looked at me with widened eyes. "I've never done either."

"Then today is your most fortunate day." I buried the battle-ax in one of the logs and then grabbed her left hand, slapping the handle of the knife in it.

"But I—"

"Are you afraid of getting your hands a little dirty?"

"Nay, but—"

"Hush, girl," I said as I spun her into my arms with her back against my chest. "I'll teach you." I snaked my arms around her body and slid my hands down her forearms to the blade. I gently pried her constricted fingers from the handle and took the dagger into my own hands.

"Beautiful, is it not? My uncle made it for me. Look how the gold and silver intertwine together. See how they twist and turn, drawing your eyes first to the contrast of their colors, but then eventually on the partnership they serve as they wrap around each other in blended beauty. And not to say that silver and gold are best only together, but there's also nothing distasteful or frightening about their congruent existence. 'Tis a stunning piece of artisan talent, wouldn't you say?"

I could tell her breath was caught as I remained close for quite a long time. It wasn't the kind of instruction necessary to learn the skills of filleting a fish, but she liked the lesson, as far as I could ascertain.

"Now to begin, you must forget all you think you know about weapons and how to wield them. Hold the knife with a gentle yet steady hand, as opposed to the steel grip you had before. Then find a good smooth rock to lay the fish upon, hold it by the tail, and skim the blade just below the layer of scales with one long stroke. Do so until all the scales are removed, but be careful not to go too deep or you'll cut away the meat. Understand?"

"I think so. But what about its head?" She scrunched her nose in disgust.

I released her and gave her backside one solid swat as I walked away. "Chop it off."

Leif's eyes flashed open, and he sat frozen on the floor of his bedroom. The dagger in his hand was the exact weapon he'd just envisioned showing a woman how to fillet a fish with. A woman who looked like Lorraine, smelled like Lorraine, and felt like Lorraine in his arms.

Grabbing his notebook where he'd jotted down facts and mapped out his ancestral lineage, he searched for a man who was a tenth-century blacksmith and craftsman. Flipping through his notes, he came upon the last names written on the page, the place where his research had ended. *Magnus, brother of Rælik, son of Baldur.*

If what Lorraine and Patrick said were true, and he was Dægan, son of Rælik, then Magnus Baldurssen could very well be his uncle, and perhaps the man who'd crafted the dagger.

He sat back, thinking. Names and dates didn't lie. The surnames matched up. Could it be?

Leif closed his eyes and took a deep breath to calm himself. There it was again: the smell of rain.

Patrick's words echoed around him. *"What Lorraine has told you is the honest truth. There's no denying who you are. But until you go in that house and dig up the evidence for yourself, you'll never know who you used to be."*

Grabbing his flashlight, brushes, and shovel, he plunged back into the hole. All night without sleep, he lay on his belly searching, sifting, and digging. He lost all sense of time and didn't stop to rest or eat. The only thing he had to stop to do was change the batteries and empty his bladder. He labored for days on end and ignored the deprivation of sleep racking his body.

About to give up, he rolled to his back in exhaustion and stared at the floor joists above him. A layer of sweat and dirt covered him from head to toe, and nothing felt more comfortable than closing his eyes and sleeping right where he was. Forcing his eyes open, he felt as if the wood supports were what it would feel like if he were lying in a coffin.

I am in a coffin, imprisoned by an overzealous dream. There is nothing else buried here, he tried to convince himself. He was finished. His mind was weary, his muscles fatigued.

Struggling to roll over on his belly and creep his way out, he staked his shovel in the dirt to tow his dog-tired body toward the opening. But it hit something. With a little more heart, he drove it in a second time and unmistakably felt the tip of the blade strike something below the surface.

Too tired and desperate to care about proper archaeological procedure, he dug away the soil in large clumps. By rights, he should have gotten bombarded with a cloud of dry dust and dirt filling his lungs, but the only thing he could smell was rain.

Clear, clean, refreshing rain.

He reached into the soil and wrapped his hands around something pliable, unearthing it without thinking about the damage he could do to something as old and fragile as a thousand-year-old relic. As he held what seemed to be a leather satchel, he wormed on his elbows to the opening and climbed out.

Sunlight, streaming in from his bedroom windows, pierced his eyes as he lay the ancient shoulder bag on the plastic and carefully opened the flap. Reaching inside, he pulled out a leather-bound book with an encasement that had seen better days and blew dust off the top. His hands shook as he divided the book and laid it open in his lap. Brightly colored hand-drawn pictures of saints, holy men, and a haloed infant adorned the pages. Stylized handwriting, similar to calligraphy, embellished the rest. Every vellum page was without smudges, blemishes, or age. He'd found the book of which Lorraine had spoken.

Closing his eyes, he let his mind wander and his memory take shape.

"No one knows of this space, Mara, save you. I built this after my longhouse was erected, so I could dig a hole in the floor without anyone knowing. 'Twas what my father did to protect this book, and it proved to be the best way of keeping it a secret."

"Why would a book need be kept in secret?"

"Because of its value," I said. "In sentiment as well as its weight in silver." I reached low inside the dark hole and pulled up an old leather satchel weathered by time. I held it as though it were a fragile newborn babe and blew the dust from its top. "This, love, is what saved my family years ago—twice even."

"Saved your family from what?"

I carried it over to the edge of the box-bed and sat down, staring at its sacred packaging. "From starvation."

Mara sat up straighter. "How does a book keep anyone from starving?"

"Before I tell you how, you should first know that I used to have another brother. A twin brother named Domaldr."

The name caught Leif by surprise. The vision that overcame him dissipated, and he remembered how Patrick had mentioned Domaldr in his rant. He had to know more.

Burying his nose in the book, he drew in a long breath of the scent of rain and allowed his buried memories to come forth.

"One day, my father awoke to a warm, sunny morning. He looked out over the fjords and the ice on the sea was beginning to melt, far sooner than usual. To father, 'twas a sign. And fortunately for all of us, he took a chance. He ventured out onto the crusted sea, braving freezing winds and floating ice. He journeyed alone in a small fishing boat around the entire southern perimeter of Norway until he could sail northeast toward Gokstad. There, he traded his last possession: this book."

"He traded it?" Mara asked. "To whom?"

"A holy man. My father had heard of his conversion to your Christian religion and knew he was probably the only one who would know its worth."

"Did he?"

"And then some. My father came back with a new crew of men, a bigger boat, and enough food and wool for three winters."

"One book did all that?"

"Ah, but 'tis not just any book, love," I said, scooting closer. "This book is said to have survived both a downpour of rain and a watery grave in the Lough Ree, yet its pages remain as dry as the day it was written."

"And you believe that?"

"I should be asking why you don't. 'Twas your Saint Ciarán who first possessed the book. If I remember correctly, the story goes that he was sitting on a bench outside the monastery of Clonmacnoise reading from this very book, when visitors came. Like a good host, he fed and gave rooms to his traveling friends and forgot all about the open book he'd left on the bench. That night, it rained like never before, but in the morning when he rushed out to retrieve the book he thought ruined, all the pages were dry, even the place in the grass

beneath the bench where the book had lain."

"You and your stories, Dægan."

"Do you not like them?"

"I do, but you're so well versed in telling them that 'tis hard to differentiate tales from the truth."

"Fine. I shall stop."

"You cannot stop now. What about the watery grave you spoke of?" Mara asked skeptically.

"'Tis also said that this man was on a boat on the Lough Ree with many other dedicated followers. The book was still in its satchel, but one of the monks was careless and dropped it over the side of the boat, where it sank to the bottom of the gray lake. To Ciarán's disappointment, he left the water that day empty-handed. Time passed, and one afternoon, the cattle, being hot from the summer sun, waded in the cool water of the Lough Ree. As one of the cows came out, the satchel was tangled around its leg. When Ciarán saw this, he rushed toward the cow and unhooked it, finding the book untouched by the water."

Mara gave me a sideways glance. "As a child, my mother told me that story, but I thought 'twas just a good fireside tale. Surely that couldn't have really happened."

"How is it that you doubt the existence of a magical book, but not of your Christ rising from the dead after three days?"

"Because Christ's rising was called forth by God Himself. With all due respect, Dægan, this book is just legend, and your father was fortunate enough that someone believed in that foolishness."

"Foolishness, aye?"

"I'm afraid so," Mara said, nodding.

"Then open it."

Mara scoffed. "Well, of course it shall be dry. You had it stored beneath your floor for many years. My opening it after all this time will prove nothing."

"Open it," I said again. "If you can read, then open it."

Mara sighed and took the satchel from my hands, laying it in her lap. I watched her, knowing the smell of aged leather filled her nostrils, as did the faint smell of rain. She paused, taking in another breath, and furrowed her brow.

My grin smeared to one side. "Cannot imagine why anyone would smell rain on a starry night like tonight."

"I never said that I smelled rain."

"You didn't have to. I know you smell it. Everyone does when they hold the book."

Mara ripped open the satchel and pulled it out. "You must be out of your mind, Dægan. I—I..." Her mouth dropped slightly. "I do smell rain."

"Now open it," I commanded.

She flipped through the pages quickly and found that every page was dry, unsmeared, and perfectly legible. She read a few lines from the middle of the page. "This is a book of the Gospels, Dægan."

Like a dam bursting under pressure, Leif's memories flooded back. He remembered searching for the book on the Isle of Man and almost dying in the process. He remembered how he'd returned home with it and gathered his father's people for the daunting exodus ahead of them. He remembered how he'd settled upon Inishmore and dug beneath his longhouse to hide it. And, more importantly, he remembered Mara, his beautiful wife, with whom he shared the sentimental book.

An elated smile gradually tugged on his lips. He'd broken free from the shackles of his ignorance and was rewarded with the most joyous feeling in his heart. He was liberated by the past he'd repressed for so long.

Leif had uncovered the missing link of his ancestral lineage where the roots of his family tree had stopped. If not for Lorraine and Patrick, he would've likely gone his whole life carrying around a notebook with an empty bracket.

He grabbed a pencil and his notebook, and filled in the name DÆGAN RÆLIKSEN below RÆLIK (Son of Baldur). And beside his past-life name, he wrote MARA (Princess of Connacht).

He leaned back and admired the way the names looked, as though they were meant to be written together, ageless through history like Romeo and Juliet. He thought about how Lorraine would enjoy the cliché and suddenly panicked.

What day is it?

He had no idea. For all he knew, a week could've have gone by and Lorraine was back in the States. Jumping to his feet, he stuffed St. Ciarán's book of the Gospels back in its satchel and tore out of his bedroom, running into Kristoff in the hallway.

"Whoa, slow down, Leif."

Leif could barely contain himself. "What day is it?"

Kristoff stared at him, gawking at his appearance.

Leif shook him. "What day is it!"

"It's Monday." He grimaced, waving his hand in front of his nose. "Time for you to take a shower."

"I don't have time," Leif muttered as he tried to squeeze past.

Kristoff grabbed him by the arm. "Where are you going?"

"I have to see Lorraine. I have to get to her before she leaves!"

"Like this?" Kristoff sneered, gesturing over Leif's dirt-ridden body.

Leif skirted into his bathroom and took a gander at himself in the mirror. His hair was clumped together with sweat and mud, his hands were soiled, his lashes were dusted with dirt, and his clothes stained.

He couldn't go to her in this fashion, but he feared he'd be too late if he showered. There wasn't time for preparation. Patrick was a man of his word, and he knew he had to stop her from leaving Ireland. Somehow, someway, he had to get to her and let her know he believed she was the reincarnated Mara and he was her husband, reborn in the same lifetime, destined to be together for all eternity.

Leif rejected the thought of cleaning up and sped from the bathroom, his heart in his throat at the thought of missing his only chance to catch Lorraine before she left Ireland.

Kristoff called to him as he fled out the door. "What the hell are you doing?"

Leif smiled as he sprinted up the road. "I'm going to marry Lorraine."

Chapter Twenty-nine

Lorraine zipped her suitcase and looked at Patrick. She noticed that from the moment they had awakened this morning, he checked his watch repeatedly. They had eight hours left before they had to be at the airport, and there was no sign of Leif.

"Are you ready?" he asked solemnly.

She had every reason not to be ready. She was about to leave Leif behind without saying good-bye. Patrick had encouraged her to be patient, to let Leif come to his senses and return on his own accord. In truth, she thought he would, even if it were only to say his farewell. She'd put all her faith in that little thread of hope, only to be disappointed. Her dreams of spending the rest of her days with Leif had shattered, and she was devastated. She had no hope left.

Patrick embraced her around the shoulders. "Come on. Mr. Flanagan's waiting outside with his carriage. He'll take us to the pier."

No matter what she felt for Leif, she had to let him go. She couldn't force him to love her, and she didn't want him to pretend. Perhaps it was better she didn't see his face as she left the isle. She might run to him and beg for his love, which would only be a pathetic and embarrassing sight.

Fighting back her tears, she grabbed her suitcase from the bed and started toward the door, when all of a sudden the door burst open. Leif rushed in, his blue eyes wide and his hair an unruly mess of dirt and tangles. A dusty, three-day-old beard shadowed his jaw. He looked larger than she remembered, and his shoulders nearly filled the span of the doorway.

For once, she feared him, intimidated by his unexpected presence. She swallowed out of nervousness and prepared to be tongue-lashed for all the hurt she'd caused him and all the drama she'd brought into his life. She anticipated that he'd carry on about how he regretted ever meeting her and how he wished like hell he wouldn't have allowed her into his heart.

But he didn't.

Instead, he stood there, trembling. He looked as if he'd forgotten how to speak.

"We were just leaving," Patrick said, stepping forward.

Leif's gaze deflected from her to Patrick and back again. "Please don't leave."

Lorraine melted as his plea came out in a weak whisper, hardly fitting for a man of his physique. Every part of her wanted to accept his request, but Patrick wasn't as generous.

"You're too late. I'm taking her home."

"Her home is here, on Inishmore. It always has been."

Lorraine caught the subtle reference Leif made to the past, her past. She squeezed Patrick's hand, an unspoken gesture to hear Leif out. She tried not to get her hopes up and looked to her best friend for guidance.

Patrick returned his focus to Leif. "It's not that simple, and you know it."

Leif breathed slowly, preparing his words. "I know who am. I'm Dægan, son of Rælik."

Patrick shook his head. "They're mere utterances, spoken words which entitle you to nothing."

Leif ignored him and continued. "I fell in love with you on the River Shannon and we married on the cliffs of Inishmore within the fort walls of Dún Aonghasa."

"Again, Leif, you're only stating words Lorraine wants to hear. It's over. We're leaving."

Leif grabbed Patrick by the shirt and spun him around, throwing him out the door. Lorraine hadn't seen that coming any more than Patrick had, and she backed up as Leif turned the lock.

When he faced her, his eyes softened immediately. "I don't mean to frighten you, Raine." He stepped toward her slowly, gazing over every inch of her body. And not out of lust, but out of scrutiny, as if he were making an identification.

She felt uncomfortable enduring his thorough inspection, and stiffened at the approach of his dirty hands. As she had nowhere to go, his arms wrapped around her, pulling her into his embrace.

"Why are you so filthy, Leif? And why do you look at me this way?"

He smiled as if pleased by her questions. "Can a husband not drown in his wife's eyes whilst she holds him?"

His familiar words sent shivers down her spine. They were the same ones Dægan offered after he'd saved her from his twin brother. Was it possible Leif remembered?

She hesitated to believe so.

"Look at me," he whispered. "Listen closely to what I say to you, for there's not much time. You first gave yourself to me in Hlymrekr. And the next morning, I thought you regretted it, but you didn't. I can describe every part of you if you want me to. I can tell you how sweet your tongue is after you've sucked the sugar from my finger. I can count on one hand the times I made love to you and wish on my very life 'twere more. I can speak of the solitary freckle just beneath your right breast and the birthmark on your inner thigh, for only a husband could know such intimate things. I'm your husband. I want naught more than your love and trust right now, and by the great God in Heaven, I wish I could steal it. But I won't. I'll wait forever and a day for you. Listen to my words, Mara, for I speak as a lost sheep. Find me. Find me in your heart...*I just might be there*."

Lorraine stood frozen in Leif's arms. He'd addressed her as Mara and eloquently spoken the very words her husband, Dægan, had uttered that one fateful day as fluently as if he'd made them up himself. No one was there the day Dægan had revealed that lyrical list of details. No one but she could understand the significance of those words. No one, save her and Dægan.

With tentative hands, she cupped Leif's grubby face and gazed into his eyes. "Is it really true? You remember?"

He clasped her hands in his and kissed her knuckles. "Aye, m'lady," he muttered before dropping to his knees. "I love you. Like the relentless rain from the Erin sky, my love will always be. For you, Mara, and no other."

Again, her heart leapt as he rattled off the sentimental words from their past. There was no doubt Leif finally remembered being the Norse warrior from a previous life. She could see it in the tumultuous storm of his eyes. She'd drowned in those eyes enough times to know.

"But how?" she asked. "What made you believe?"

He stood up and slipped the leather strap over his head, then handed her a dusty leather satchel. At first, she didn't recognize it, wondering how she'd missed seeing the shoulder bag hanging from his side the whole time. Then the beautiful effervescent scent of rain struck her.

"You found it?" She gasped, unable to believe her own eyes. "You dug up St. Ciarán's book?"

"Yes," he breathed. "It was right where you said it was."

She heard the fatigue in his voice and finally understood the layer of dirt covering him. "Is this what you've been doing for the past days? Digging?"

He nodded. "I had to. You were going to leave me. And I loved you too much to let you walk out of my life."

"Oh, Leif," she cried, hugging him tightly. He picked her up, and she buried her face in the solid wall of his chest. She relished the feel of his arms around her and couldn't care less about the flurry of dirt that puffed from his shirt. She felt precious in his embrace and savored holding tight to her modern-day hero.

"I could die right now—right here—and be a happy man."

The huskiness of his voice played a sinful melody in her ears, and the velvet caress of his lips on her neck played havoc over her entire body. He set her on her feet and brushed a loose strand of hair from her face, gazing into her eyes.

"Marry me, Raine, and make me a jubilant man."

****

Lorraine stood in front of the mirror as Maggie Flanagan applied the finishing touches of island flowers in her hair. She couldn't believe this day had come. Only a few hours ago, she'd thought her time in Ireland was coming to an abrupt end. Now, she was about to leap into forever with a man she'd dreamed about since she was a little girl on an island she held dear. Not many could boast finding their soulmates within a lifetime. She was blessed with finding her soulmate in two lifetimes. It was, indeed, a blessing of huge proportion.

"There," Maggie said, examining her work. "What do you think?"

Lorraine gazed over the way Maggie had curled her hair in loose ringlets and adorned her forehead with a crown of purple and yellow blossoms. Reminiscent of the first time she'd married, the flowers added the right amount of color to her simple, elegant gown. Nothing about her attire was elaborate, but it was perfect nonetheless. She didn't need complexities or high-dollar appeal to make this day special. Just knowing Leif was waiting for her in the very spot they had once pledged their love and fidelity more than a thousand years ago made her heart sing.

She turned and looked at Maggie. "I love what you've done. Thank you."

Maggie smiled and began fiddling with Lorraine's hair a bit more. "You know, you and I are very fortunate women. We've fallen for exceptional men, don't you think?"

Lorraine listened intently, eager to hear more of the woman's praise, and more importantly, the way she felt about Kristoff.

"I know you may not know this, but Kristoff and Leif came to my rescue a few nights ago." Maggie's smile faded. "I'd been attacked by two men outside the pub, and if not for Leif and Kristoff's bravery...well, let's just say I was able to walk away with my dignity because of them."

Lorraine was speechless. "I'm so sorry that happened

to you. I had no idea."

"I'm not sorry," Maggie concluded. "If not for that night, my brother would have never seen the side of Kristoff that I knew was there all along. Nor would he have allowed me to see him again."

Lorraine took Maggie by the shoulders and looked her in the eye. "Kristoff likes you very much too."

An uncertain smile flitted across Maggie's lips. "He does?"

Lorraine nodded. "I know he does."

A pounding at the door interrupted their quiet conversation. "Come on, ladies," Kristoff called on the other side. "We're burning daylight here."

The two women laughed. "We're coming," Maggie answered back.

"Make certain you save some of those flowers for the funeral tonight. My brother's going to kill me for not having you at the fort on time."

Maggie rolled her eyes at Kristoff's joke. "Are you ready?"

Lorraine took a deep breath and smiled. "I've never been more ready."

Unexpectedly, Maggie hugged her. "Thank you for allowing me to be here. I know we don't know each other very well," she said, glancing in the direction of the man behind the door. "But I'm hoping time will change that."

"I'm very certain we'll have plenty of time to get to know each other."

The door flew open, and an impatient Kristoff glared. "Seriously girls, if you don't hurry up—" Upon seeing Lorraine, his eyes softened and a slow grin teased his lips. "Wow. You look beautiful, Raine."

"Of course, she does," Maggie said. "She's the bride. She's supposed to make every other woman in the world pale in comparison to her on this day. Now, roll your tongue back in your mouth and help us to the carriage."

Kristoff tripped, making haste to assist Lorraine in her heels. He offered his left arm to Lorraine and his right to Maggie. "I'm assuming you're attending this wedding with *me*, right?"

Maggie slipped her arm through his. "Well, I didn't get all dressed up for my brother."

"Speaking of," Kristoff interjected as he proudly guided them both out of the Man of Aran Cottage to the decorated horse and cart outside. "You think Flanagan will finally let me kiss you in public?"

"Have you forgotten who my brother is?" Maggie warned. "He thinks he's been generous letting you escort me to the wedding, and I think you'd be wise not to push your luck."

Kristoff's smile turned devilish. "Oh, you've got a lot to learn about me, Red."

****

Leif stood at the cliffs of Inishmore within the nostalgic ruins of Dún Aonghasa, and he was nervous. Not about marrying Lorraine, but that she hadn't showed up yet. He'd given Kristoff strict instructions to escort her to the fort by horse and carriage. Surely his brother wouldn't let him down when it mattered most.

He glanced at his watch—*ten minutes late*—then sighed. Patrick, who stood beside him at the altar, laughed. "What's so funny?" Leif asked.

"Just never thought I'd ever see the day when Dægan

Ræliksen wasn't so sure of himself."

"What if she doesn't show? What if she's changed her mind?"

"It's the wedding she's waited for all her life," Patrick consoled. "She'll be here."

Leif tried to remain confident that Lorraine wouldn't leave him standing at the altar. He then found other things to fret about. "How do I look?" he asked, smoothing his hands down his front as gusts of wind blew the bearskin cloak he'd chosen to don across his shoulders.

Patrick looked him over. "Ridiculous."

"Shut up," Leif retorted. "Raine will appreciate it."

"She'll be the only one."

Leif grimaced as he was forced to stand beside the man who loved Lorraine as much as he did himself. If it were his choice, he would have rather proceeded with the wedding without Patrick's presence. But it wasn't his to make. Lorraine had asked him to witness the union, and he couldn't argue differently given the effort Patrick had made to get them together.

"I've been thinking," Leif murmured.

"About?"

"About us. About you. It doesn't seem fair that we're keeping a secret from Lorraine. I think she'd like to know who you are. She has a right to know—"

"No," Patrick interrupted, his eyes stern. "She can't know who I am."

"Why not?"

"Because then she'd feel like she'd have to make a choice. Do not make her choose, Leif. That's cruel." He paused. "Believe me, it's not that I'm afraid she'll pick you over me. I *know* who her choice would be, and I can live with that. But it's not fair to make her have to choose. Look," he said, softening his voice. "I've spent two lifetimes thinking about this. All I've ever wanted was to make her happy. Don't spoil my only chance to do so."

Leif found it difficult to look Patrick in the eye. Knowing he was to hold his tongue and keep a secret from the woman he was about to marry left a hard knot in the pit of his stomach. It was clear Patrick was the better man for being so selfless, and he almost thought Patrick deserved her more. Almost.

Pushing those thoughts aside, he checked his watch again. "What is taking her so long?"

Patrick chuckled. "Calm down. You're not the only one who's been left to sweat bullets at the altar waiting for her. Trust me, she'll be here, and afterward, it will be worth the wait."

Leif gave him a sideways glance, noting the huge smile on his face. He loathed knowing that Patrick had also consummated a wedding night with her. "Wipe that grin off your face."

"Sorry. There're just some memories a man can't forget."

"You know, I could've gone my whole life without being reminded of the intimacies you once shared with her."

Patrick patted him on the back. "You didn't think I'd let you get off that easily."

"How can you do this?" Leif said, unable to fully understand Patrick's selflessness. "How can you stand here and offer the woman you love to someone else without resentment?"

"Because I know that someone else is you. And you're the kind of man who's going to love her the way she deserves to be loved from this day forth." Patrick cleared his throat, turning sentimental. "You're a great man, Leif. You always were."

Leif didn't know what to say, but he found a new appreciation for Lorraine's protective friend. He still wasn't sure how the man could be so self-sacrificing. If the tables were turned, he could never give up Lorraine.

He thought longer on the regard Patrick had for him, recalling, from long ago on this very cliff's edge, the day he'd learned of greatness and God. Looking over his shoulder, he took in the sight of the sun setting in the distance. With the backdrop of a crimson sky above a sea of calm, reflective water, the scenery was both comforting and magnificent. Taking it as a sure sign of His grace, he offered a silent prayer of thanks to the one God who'd made this possible.

Leif felt a bump against his arm and glanced at Patrick, who directed him to look ahead. The sight of Lorraine making her entrance through the gap of the ringfort's dilapidated stone walls took his breath away. Her hair was let down from the usual ponytail, cascading in curls from a tiara of island flowers, and her dress was a fine gown of simple, pale green cotton, plunging low at the neckline. Her face shone like polished ivory, her lips the color of summer roses.

As she made her way up to the cliff's edge, where he, Patrick, and the priest stood waiting, he was lost in his own world, staring at the most beautiful woman he'd ever seen. Standing face-to-face, he took her hands in his and could smell her as remarkably as if she were right in his arms.

He looked down at their joined hands, and it felt as though everything at this moment was where it should be.

Lady Raine was finally his, and it was so.

Epilogue

Patrick sat on a barstool at Molly Malone's, the local Irish pub in Kentucky where Lorraine usually served drinks behind the bar. It was as empty as he'd ever seen it, though it could have been because it was only eleven o'clock on a weekday morning. But to him, it was more than empty. It was absent Lorraine.

Her replacement, the new female bartender, leaned on her elbow and cocked her head. "Did you figure out what you wanted to order?"

Patrick sighed. Lorraine wouldn't even have to ask. She'd know his usual drink was a Coors Lite, and it would be sitting in front of him before he could even say hello.

"I'll take a shot of Southern Comfort, hundred proof."

"Sure thing," she muttered as she left to prepare it.

"Hundred proof, huh? That's a little out of your league."

The familiar voice from behind caused him to twist in his seat, and he was shocked to see Beth walk into the dimly lit joint. She hardly gave him a second look as she sat beside him. It had been several weeks since he'd returned from Ireland, and he'd never let Beth know he was back. He assumed she wouldn't care after what he'd done to her. By all rights, he was no better than Brad for choosing Lorraine's call over hers.

He knew he'd hurt her, and he'd every intention of one day apologizing for his mistake. But he hadn't prepared himself for it today.

"How was your trip?" she asked, breaking the awkward silence.

Patrick closed his eyes. He heard the hint of sarcasm in her question and couldn't believe she insisted on making small talk. "It was eventful, to say the least."

"The wedding? Or that Lorraine found the love of her life with your help?"

He looked at her now. "How did you know?"

Beth stared into the mirror behind the bar. "I stopped by your mother's this morning. She told me."

"Oh," was all he could muster, and he turned back around. He was shocked she'd even made the effort to follow up on his well-being. He figured it would be a cold day in hell before she ever spoke to him again.

Thankfully, the bartender brought his stout shot of whiskey. Beth ordered her usual Bud Light and turned to watch Patrick as he touched the glass with tentative fingers.

He felt her eyes boring into him. "What?"

"You think if you drink, you'll forget her?" Beth asked directly.

"I'd like to forget," Patrick admitted somberly. "Whatever it takes."

He felt Beth's touch upon his hand. He didn't have to look at her to know she somehow pitied him. He couldn't stand it. Any of it. It ate at him to know Beth was still hanging on, despite how he'd left things between them. Right now, all he wanted was to be alone. To sulk in his misery by himself.

"Why are you here, Beth?"

"I'm here because you need me. Now more than ever."

He wanted to laugh. What he needed was for someone to erase his memory. To expunge every recollection he ever had of Lorraine—of Mara. Getting on that plane bound for Cincy had been the second hardest thing he'd ever had to do. The first was watching Leif and Lorraine kiss as husband and wife at the ceremony. He'd give anything to remove that image from his memory and wished it was as easy as getting drunk.

"Please don't take this personally, but I just want to be left alone."

Before he could lift the shot to his lips, Beth plucked it from his hand and moved it out of his reach. "You don't need this. Nor do you need Lorraine. What you need is a good smack upside the head."

Patrick couldn't argue. "Go ahead. I deserve it. Take your best shot."

Beth smiled and shook her head. "Not because you broke your promise, or left the country without so much as a word. But because you don't remember who I am. Who I used to be."

Patrick swiveled his barstool to look at her. "And...who are you?"

"It's funny how the mind works. How the brain can't remember certain faces or memories even when the person stares you in the face."

"What are you talking about, Beth?"

"Perhaps this will help you remember." She sat up straighter and prepared her words. "I can make you forget all about her. Stop dreaming of what can never be, and take what you want from what is real—flesh and blood. Lorraine, by her own vows to another man, denies you what you long for. I'll never deny you, Patrick. Or should I call you Breandán Mac Liam?"

Patrick's heart stopped. He brushed back Beth's dark

hair and examined every detail of her face as his memory started to filter back. "Sorcha?"

Beth smiled and slipped off her stool, snuggling up against his chest. She captured his frozen gaze and wrapped her arms around him. "Yes. It's me…"

THE END

Author's Note

If you enjoyed *Souls Reborn*, I encourage you to try *Tempered Steel,* the fourth book in the *Vikings of Honor Series*. The story takes place at the moment *Emerald Glory* ends, giving you the continuing story of Dægan's oldest brother Gustaf and his lover, Æsa.

Tempered Steel

Gustaf Ræliksen lives by the blade of his sword. After avenging his father's murder and reuniting with his family, he wants nothing more than to settle down and have sons of his own. Only one woman will do—a beautiful redheaded thrall he saved from the spoils of war.

Free from slavery and those who kept her captive, Æsa has nothing to offer the noble warrior except her heart. But when someone with a deep score to settle seeks revenge and the whereabouts of buried silver that only Æsa knows, she must break Gustaf's heart in order to spare his life.

Gustaf's world is torn asunder, and he has but one vow— saving the woman he loves from the dangerous rival who will stop at nothing to have it all.

If you enjoyed this book by Renee Vincent, please consider leaving an honest review at your favorite vendor. Reviews not only give credibility to an author's work, they also help other readers find quality books worth reading.

About Renee Vincent

RENEE VINCENT is a *USA Today* bestselling author of romance and women's fiction. Her books have earned numerous accolades, including a #1 Bestseller for Viking Romance.

She lives on a secluded hundred-acre horse farm in the rolling hills of Kentucky with her husband, two beautiful daughters, and a few fur babies who've managed to weasel their way into a couple of books. When she's not writing, she loves to decorate (and redecorate) her home, knit cozy blankets, send homemade cards to family and friends, and concoct her own versions of recipes to pass down to her girls.

Through the years, Renee has connected with some of the most dedicated and gracious readers who crave unpredictable plot twists, gripping adventure, and undying love. For that, she is most grateful.

www.ReneeVincent.com

Books By Series

Vikings of Honor Series
Sunset Fire, Book 1
Emerald Glory, Book 2
Souls Reborn, Book 3
Tempered Steel, Book 4

Mavericks of Meeteetse Series
Longing for Langston, Brody & Liv, Book 1
Made for McKinley, Jonas & Ava, Book 2
Falling For Forester, Cole & Crys, Book 3

Jamett & Joseph Series
The Start of Something Good, Book 1
The Road to Something Better, Book 2
The Gift of Something Grand, Book 3
Something's Bound to Happen, Books 1 – 3

Stand Alone Novel
Silent Partner

ReneeVincent.com